C A Z

CHURCH
AGAINST
ZOMBIES

Alathia Paris Morgan

Table of Contents

Acknowledgments

To Dana, Every time you continue to go above and beyond.
Thank you.
Rebel Edit & Design
Book cover: Nicole Paris, I was doubly blessed with you!
Adobe Stock: cover photo purchased

The Against Zombies Series:
Moms Against Zombies Book1—Emma Jackson and Trish
Walsh's story
Military Against Zombies Book 2—Brad Jackson, Patti Jackson,
Linc Harris' story
Co-Ed's Against Zombies Book 3—River Weaver, Stacy Morris,
Angela Richard's story
Churches Against Zombies Book 4—Cole Jackson and River
Weaver's Story,
Carson Walsh's story, Andi Jackson.
Geeks Against Zombies Book 5—Sean, Caleb and Finn's story
Governments Against Zombies Book 6—Cooper Walsh

Jackson Family Tree

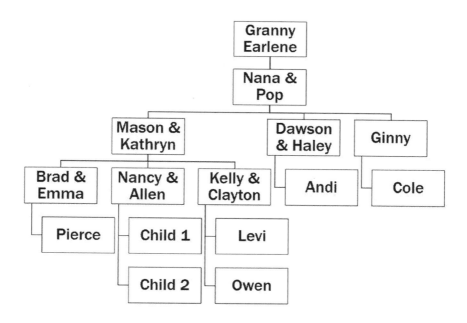

Prologue

Three months since people first became infected.

Welcome to KLIVE Radio, the only radio station brought to you by the Church Against Zombies. If you're hearing this commercial and feel that you're alone, we understand. Churches are supposed to be a place of hope, and this is the only church radio station that will help you survive the zombies.

Those infected by the illness that came through the world have taken out many of the living in our cities and rural areas. If you are stuck in a home or building with a landline, please call 555-555-0000 for help relocating to a stable area that has been cleared of Zombie Infected Things, or ZITs. Most of those in our listening area can be rescued by one of our groups or the military that is operating in the area.

If you are forced to leave the place that you have been staying, then make sure that you have a weapon that can hit the brain on an infected body. This will guarantee that the infected is dead. It may take more than one hit to ensure that the ZIT isn't going to bite you on the ankle.

Plans are in place to have things running again in the city in the next several months, and we can use everyone's help in doing this. We need people who have knowledge in all sorts of jobs, or we can teach you so that we can turn the lights back on in our portion of the world.

Here's some music to bring us all together in as a united force against the zombies. Stay tuned for updates on the hour, and with tips for how to survive during this zombie apocalypse every thirty minutes.

Chapter 1

Back on the Farm

Trish

I loved my family, and enjoyed the time we were getting to spend on the farm, mostly worry free. But after weeks into this new world, it was starting to drive me crazy.

"Linc, I need to get off the farm. Is there any way that I can come with you when you go to get the solar panels?" I broached the subject several weeks after he moved into the main house with Jessica.

He blushed, and turned to find her unloading the truck full of vegetables into the barn.

"I was kind of hoping that you might let her go with me." He looked so apologetic about asking again.

I knew they were in love, but I was ready to plead my case and give him no choice in the matter.

"Look here, I love that you and Jessica have found each other. It's wonderful. I certainly don't mind that you're both wrapped up with each other and I'm on my own with six kids a lot. This isn't about that. I need to get away. Cooper threw us into this situation, and while I'm sure he's fine, I honestly need to find a way to do something that will keep my mind off of where he's at and what he's doing."

"Makes sense, but you know he wants you to stay safe. Going with me would certainly not fall under that category." Linc smiled, thinking that he'd made a valid argument.

"Yes, you're so right. He would want me safe, and right now, my sanity is about gone. It's time for someone to travel to the city and bring back a little piece of the world with them. We've managed to keep our kids and the ones in town busy with chores, yet they can only work the same puzzles or play the same games so many times.

"Beth can't go because when she got back, all of her store would be empty. She's given me a list, though, and I think I can get most of it at a couple different places. It'll help with community spirit, and give the moms a chance to distract the children."

"You're not trained like the guys—" Linc started to protest.

"Uh-uh, no way. You know I can handle a gun or the backside of a hoe. You can't take all the guys from the farm with you, and the guys from town that you have going with you were businessmen that you've taught to take down infected."

"Okay, but I want you to write a letter to Cooper in case you die that I protested and you overruled me."

"Done. I'll have it in your hands before we leave in the morning." I refrained from jumping up and down.

"Jessica's going to be disappointed that she's not going with me."

"You let me worry about her. The plus side of that is you don't need to be distracted with having her there, and you'll have a reason for making it home alive." I left him standing on the porch so that I could pack my bag. If only explaining it to the kids and convincing them was as easy as Linc had been.

"Mommy, don't leave us." Trevor started to cry.

"I'll bring you back some new toys to play with," I promised, knowing that it would stop his fit.

"Can I make a list of stuff I need for you to get,

Mom?" Joy's face lit up.

"You may, but I might not be able to get everything you put on it, but I'll do my best. I plan to find something that each of you will enjoy."

"How long will you be gone? Is it still okay if I spend the night over at Katie's house?" Nicole questioned.

"Aunt Jessica should be fine with that, assuming that you do all your chores and behave for her as well. I'll be gone a few days, maybe a week. It will depend on where we have to go and how long it takes to load things up safely."

Nicole and Joy both hugged me a little longer, but Trevor's lip was still trembling. "Don't you get deaded, Mommy. I loves you so much."

Listening to the kids, I knew that they were concerned about this trip, and it only made sense. But in this new world, it was a necessity.

I tucked each kid in for the night and went to do the perimeter check before Tyler took over. I'd volunteered for the eight o'clock to midnight shift so that I'd be out of the house when Linc and Jessica were saying goodnight to each other.

Everything looked normal, so I stopped to rest on the fence that faced the road and our nearest neighbors.

Seeing Linc and Jessica in the first stages of love made me realize how much I missed my husband. He could be so annoying, but he was always there for me, and this was the longest we'd been apart in years.

We were blessed that he'd seemed to have an idea that this might be coming and prepared a safe place for us. The farm was so far out in the country that it had been ignored by most of the traffic coming from the cities.

There were still a few dead walking around that we'd find, but once the town had gotten rid of it's horrible leader, they'd cleared out a good fifty miles around of single or groups of dead.

It hadn't been easy, and we'd learned the hard way that farm work and infected dead trying to attack weren't a good thing, but there was always a learning curve when something like this happened.

Linc had gotten the area farms back to running safely, and there were a few of the smaller towns in the area that had formed a militia of their own. This had helped when large groups made their way to the barriers, and extra people with guns were sent to contain the threat.

Cooper had always had that take-charge personality, but right now, I just wanted a pair of arms to hold me so I could let go for just a few minutes. I hoped that our little excursion would be enough to curb the restlessness that was starting to give me insomnia.

The buzzer on my watch beeped. It was time for another walk around the fences. At least we would be the generation of the fit because the zpoc had made us get off of our asses and exercise.

I didn't want Linc to have any regrets in bringing me on the trip to gather supplies.

The backroads had been cleaned of all immobile cars so the roads were clear, until we reached the edge of the Backroads Coalition (as we'd begun to call our group). We knew there were other groups out there, but so far, we hadn't found more than a person or two alive.

I was driving a large, white paneled van that had *Freddie's Fresh Bread* painted on the side with a spray-painted line through it. We didn't want anyone trying to highjack the truck for bread, not that it would stop a crazy person or any of the dead. It just felt safer.

A huge downside to this zombie apocalypse thing was that there were no radio stations playing. We had a lending library of CDs now that were passed around between everyone because it was really quiet when we had to drive without radios. There were some things that you never thought about being important until they were suddenly gone.

They had sandwiched my truck in the middle of three others that were going to bring back supplies other than solar panels. Our main goal was to get the staples: toilet paper, baby items, clothes, female items, canning jars, and puzzles.

If there was food anywhere available, we'd certainly take that, but those in the city would have taken most of it to survive. We had enough fresh food, but it would have to last all winter, and we needed to find a way to store stuff in case we didn't get the solar panels installed.

We had about two more months of summer before it started to cool off. I was looking for things that weren't on the list of necessities, like water balloons and water guns. We might be in the middle of a crisis, but kids still needed to be kids and have some fun.

The train of trucks moving through the last gate had me looking around for unexpected problems. Even though we were still about thirty miles from the nearest town, I guess I was certain that we'd just be seeing the dead everywhere now that we were past the safety net.

Instead, we rolled through several small abandoned crossroad stops with only a few dead wandering around.

The shops with heavy equipment and warehouses were on the edge of the larger town, and we pulled up to a closed gate.

Tyler had accompanied Linc, while we'd left Sam and Josh with Jessica to help keep an eye on things.

He motioned the empty trucks to park on the street so that we could pull out quickly if we needed to. The drivers were supposed to stay put, and the extra men and women who'd come along were going to go inside and load up a semi full of panels to be delivered to our small town.

I knew that Linc had put ours together and seemed to understand the complexities of how they worked and what parts were needed to get everything up and running. He'd taken a crash course when Cooper had told him to move to the farm.

There were a few trucks sitting outside the warehouse that were built to transport the panels without breaking them.

"Get these loaded up. Tyler will show you how to do it. Nolan, come with me and I'll show you what I'm looking for inside." Linc handed out orders, and unless there were dead inside, they shouldn't have any problems.

Nervously, I scanned the roads in front and behind us. Even though I knew we had lookouts, it still bothered me that we were sitting out in the open like this.

Tired of listening to the CD, I hit the eject button and the truck cab was filled with music.

My hand dropped the CD in shock and I stared at the radio, hoping that I wasn't hearing imaginary voices.

The music of a country song was so refreshing that I didn't even notice the tears streaming down my face until an announcer came on.

"Well that will do it for this thirty minutes of survival tunes. We're going to have our latest tip before we start the next half hour of tunes based on our current problems—zombies."

The announcer gave a few common sense ideas about how to stay alive by only traveling during the daylight. Help others if you are able to, and call the Church Against Zombies to connect with your local community.

What the hell?

Franticly, I picked up the radio. "Linc, I have something important for you when you get done loading."

"Zombies?" came the terse question.

"No, it's not an emergency. I found a solution to

something when you have a minute."

I sank back against the seat, trying to process what I'd just heard.

Sure enough, once the service announcement was over, the familiar refrains of the Cranberries brought a chuckle to my lips.

Not only did these people who were broadcasting seem to be alive, but they had a sense of humor.

A knock on the window startled me.

Linc was standing there, impatiently waiting for me to roll the window down.

"Seriously, Trish, this is a cute joke, but I don't have time to listen to songs about zombies when they could be just a few feet away." He looked so frustrated at the interruption to the plan.

I couldn't keep the smile off my face.

"Linc, it's not a CD. That is actually playing on the radio. Here, listen..." The song ended, and a quick introduction as the next themed song started had done its job.

Linc's mouth hung open.

"Do you know what this means? There are other people out there, not only surviving, but starting over." I was excited until I saw the look of caution on his face.

"What? Aren't we going to find them?" I asked.

"Not today. We need to get these back and the other supplies that you came for. If this is a legit station, then we have a few days to come up with a plan before we go running in and get caught up in something worse than having a Jim Danvers in charge of us."

Swallowing back the happiness I'd felt only moments before, I could see the reasons why we'd need to keep this from the others. It was a good thing I hadn't told everyone over the radio.

"Promise me that we'll look into it soon."

He nodded. "Trish, I want nothing more than for all the infected to be gone, but it's going to take a lot of people working together to get things back in order. If Cooper is still alive in Washington, then we might have a chance for some order. So far, we haven't heard from him, and the world keeps falling apart. Anything we do has to be planned out before contact is made, if we even want to make contact. It could be a trap to get us to bring resources to them and they kill us."

The radio beeped. "We're loaded up."

"Be right there."

"Don't be discouraged. This is really good news, but right now, our town needs electricity, and we should get it to them before we move on to the next survival need."

"Yeah, you're right. Go get things ready so we can go shopping for my list of stuff." I tried to keep from bursting into tears. Nobody needed to deal with a weeping female while trying to keep the infected away.

Gulping in a few deep breaths, I wiped at my eyes. Moms didn't get the option of crying whenever they wanted. I could keep things going until we got back to the farm, but when I was out of danger, all bets were off that I would have a pillow soaked with tears tonight.

Things went off without a hitch, but this time, I was in charge of acquisitions when we pulled up to the back doors of the supercenter.

Tyler hopped out of one of the trucks and helped us back into the loading centers.

The trailers with the solar panels had traveled back the way we'd cleared out, and we were on the way back to the country roads where the going would be much slower. They would have a head start, but most of the extra bodies were in my group to help search and load up.

The two pickup trucks with Linc and Nolan were in the front sitting idle, revving the engines and honking the horns to draw out the undead.

The noise would attract anything that was dead in a few miles' radius, but it would clear out most of the crowds so that we could handle what was left.

I wasn't looking forward to killing any infected, but I was going to have to do it eventually.

We cut the engines as soon as we were lined up, allowing the noise out front to do its job.

Tyler motioned everyone to get ready as he opened the cargo door.

A group of about ten stumbled out, giving us a chance to stake, spike, or stab them before they hurt us. I plunged a spike through a middle-aged woman's head and used her body weight to help pull it free as she dropped to the ground.

I looked around and didn't see anything else moving.

"Pull these over to the side, out of the way, and watch where you're walking. The guts are slippery, and nobody wants to drive back smelling like that." I grinned, because as the mom of two boys and two girls, those words had never come out of my mouth before, and I thought I'd said everything in the book already.

When the other two doors were rolled up, I noticed that the sounds of the horns were growing farther away, meaning that anything that was left inside was up to us to take care of before we started shopping.

The back of the bay was filled with stacked containers on pallets. I shined the flashlight on the words, hoping to find the toilet paper. It was stacked behind the boxes of cereal, so that was a bonus. There was always fresh milk, and cereal would be a quick way to feed the kids, something that had been a part of their previous lives.

"Take the pallet jack and wheel those pallets directly onto the truck just as they are. We can cut the plastic off later, and it'll keep them from falling on top of other things in the truck."

I started marking the boxes of different stacks while they started loading them into the truck. At each swinging door, we had a lookout to make sure that there weren't any surprises that rushed us.

When we began to get full, I motioned to three of the ladies that were with us that we were going through the doors. The other things we needed were inside the store, and it wasn't likely that we'd find boxes full of them back there.

"Grab a cart and hold tight to your weapon," I spoke quietly as I pushed the door open.

It was almost totally dark, and that made what we were doing much more dangerous.

"Crap! I can't see anything, Trish," Lisa whispered next to me.

I turned the flashlight on, hoping it wouldn't attract more than we'd bargained for. "Keep our baskets next to each other. Joanne, leave your basket here and walk behind us to make sure nothing comes up that way."

The groans were still coming from the darkness, but I knew there were a lot less than we'd had before. Thankfully these superstores were setup in the same manner so we could find our way.

"Head for the toy section."

"Seriously?" Berry's voice rose in terror. "We're going toy shopping?"

"We need games and things to keep the kids occupied."

"Oh," she whimpered, moving along with the group. "I don't like this."

An infected reached out toward us and I shoved the cart into his gut. He leaned over it, and I punched the spike forward into his eye socket.

"There…see? We've got this," I spoke confidently as we turned the corner, into a stumbling group of dead.

"Back to back!" I yelled, because at this point, being quiet wasn't going to help.

"Oh my God, we're gonna die." Berry started to shake.

Transferring my flashlight to the cart, I reached over and slapped her.

"What did you do that for?" she shrieked.

"Fight or you're gonna die. Kill 'em, girls."

We waded into the groping group of dripping, smelly flesh, taking out the first line.

"Move back after you kill one so the next one will have to get over the body to get to you."

'Rinse and repeat' was the motto I kept muttering to myself. I was not going to die like this.

Shots echoed around us and the bodies we were fighting didn't seem to be fighting as hard.

"I don't know who's helping, but let's keep going."

Moments later, lights shined in my face, and I held up my hand to shield my eyes.

"Thought you could use a little help over here," Linc drawled from the other side of a pile of slimy bodies.

"Regroup on the next aisle, girls. We made it."

"I killed those things, but I'm pretty sure I broke a nail," Berry complained.

"It'll grow back," I assured her.

"Um…Trish…?" Lisa called out.

"Yeah?"

"I think I got bit," she mumbled as she slumped to the floor.

"Linc, what do we do? Is there a way to stop it from infecting her?"

"Not that I know of, but let's get her out into the light." He and Nolan picked her up and we followed behind, still on the lookout for strays.

He laid her down on the ground, out by the trucks.

"Good news, she's not bit," he announced to everyone crowding around.

"Then why is she bleeding?" Berry cried.

"She was shot."

"Are the trucks loaded?" I looked at the guys.

"Mostly," Tyler acknowledged.

"Berry, you and Joanne stay here and help Linc. The rest of us are going to go back in there for bandages and alcohol. Two of you hold the flashlights, and the rest of us will gather what we can."

"You'll be okay." I awkwardly patted her shoulder,

knowing she wouldn't have been shot if I hadn't insisted on getting the toys.

A mad dash later, we were back with random things pulled off the shelves.

"Will this work?" Tyler handed Linc a few tools to pull the bullet out, and then sew her up.

"Yep. While I'm doing this, why don't you go back in there and finish getting the last of the things on the list?" Linc saw me start to protest.

"I can't work if you're all staring at me. Besides, it'll get things off our list. Don't forget the canning jars. Go." He pointed to the door.

"All right, you heard the man. Let's do it."

Two trips later, an unconscious Lisa was placed in the back of Linc's truck.

"Close the doors so if we want to come back and get more stuff, we aren't just advertising where the good stuff is at," Tyler instructed the guys.

When I climbed into the truck and pulled into the convoy, I felt relieved. Yet if this was the kind of thing that the groups who were going out to clear each area were doing, then I wasn't sure that I wanted to be a part of it.

Maybe I would just stay home on the next trip and worry about which child was going to fall out of a tree or poke their sibling in the eye. Non-zombie problems would be a welcome change, even though the days of groaning about kid problems wasn't that far in the past.

Window rolled down with the radio playing songs about America made the miles go much faster until we made it to the secure roadblock where we could all breathe a little easier.

Chapter 2

"Everyone listen up!" Linc called the meeting to order. "We have a few things to discuss, and we need to get started so that we don't use up the daylight."

"You got the solar panels...yada yada. What else do we need to discuss?" Bert in the back yelled. "We all know that the most important people will be getting them. What do the rest of us care since we have to wait?"

"Bert, you know that's not true." Wade waved his hand in the air to get the room's attention. "From the calculations that we made today, we can put together units of three or four and power the whole block. Since we have several homes that are vacant, it'll make it where we can use the same system as the electric company to distribute it to each home."

"I'm pretty sure we could use a few volunteers to help get this going. It's going to be hands-on training so that each person can go on and do the next block, teaching someone else at the same time."

A slight grumble went through the room, but no one voiced any opposition.

"If we can get some help, I think the panels can be installed by tomorrow or the next day at the latest. We can rest and do other things around here before going back for another load. The next town over is going to get theirs done next week, so if you think you want to add electrician to your resume, now would be a good time to get some training in."

Hands went up from the youth that were present. They would use any excuse to get out of town and see other people. Their version of a barn raising from the old days when they got to have a dance after the work was done.

I smiled when Carson raised his hand, but I didn't plan to object. If he could defend the farm with a gun, there was no reason that he couldn't play with electricity while learning at the same time.

"Now that that's settled, we have one more item to discuss." Linc exchanged a glance with Wade. "When we were in the city, we were able to pick up a radio broadcast.

It seemed to be coming from Knoxville. A church has taken over the radio station, giving out survival advice to those that need it against the zombies. They're offering to rescue people who are in need."

"Why aren't we contacting them right now?" Berry waved her hand to get everyone's attention.

"That's why we're discussing our options—" Linc tried to continue, but she interrupted again.

"Honestly, I think what we did yesterday was stupid. Not the solar panels, but going into the superstore was a terrible idea. Poor Lisa had to pay the consequences."

"Um, Berry, can I ask you a personal question? Did you use the shampoo they brought back at the school today? Is it possible that you had cereal for breakfast like everyone else did?" Linc abruptly questioned.

"Yeah, so?"

"Well, you wouldn't have had any of those things if we hadn't gone into the superstore. Think of the toilet paper. We were close to using paper or rags. That's not the kind of smell that you want to have just sitting around until the electricity starts up so you can do laundry again," Tyler pointed out.

"Whatever. But you have to admit, if it hadn't been for Trish trying to get toys for the kids, then Lisa would never have gotten hurt."

"You're making it sound like doing something for the kids was a bad idea. I think you can be on the kid rotation and help out with the babies who get bored. After two days, you'll be begging to be put back on one of the other details," Joanne snapped, standing up for me.

"I'm not being selfish. I just think if we have the opportunity to connect with another group that isn't all about farms stuff, then we should take it. I for one want to transfer to the city compound."

Wade laughed out loud. "I'm sorry, Berry. The world has changed, and if we want to have food and shelter when winter comes, then everyone will have to become some sort of farmer. Those in the city don't have fresh eggs, milk, or vegetables. They're having to learn those things just like we are out here. What it would mean is that we could do some trading of goods with them and get a picture of the overall cleanup."

"The military's involved at different points across the U.S., but what we don't know is how badly each city was hit. If one in five people got infected, then that means each person has at least four dead people trying to kill them. I think we can get a few areas cleaned up, but it will take working together. We want to be cautious because we don't want to have another dictatorship that we join forces with, only to be murdered in our beds." Linc tried to explain the cons of meeting with other groups, but other than a few nods of agreement, the majority wanted to find out more about the Church Against Zombies.

"Can we agree that we need to get the solar panels up and running?" Wade interjected, getting back to the vote.

"I guess we could wait that long," Nolan offered. "The next group that goes to get more panels could see about a meeting after the trucks are loaded, and all they have to do is drive back. If something goes wrong, they can always lose them in the city and come back another way."

"Sound advice, Nolan," Linc complemented the younger man.

"Instead of trying to setup a meeting, we can take a group of about three or four guys and go over that way. If they're what they say, then they'll have a roadblock setup somewhere that we'll run across trying to get into the city," Wade suggested.

"Isn't that just like the leadership around here? Always trying to get the best of everything, you'll come back and sugarcoat it. If you all leave, you might not be in charge when you get back," Bert threatened.

Tyler smiled. "That's why you're going to be one of the ones to go meet this Church Against Zombies."

"I'm not a zombie killer, though. I wouldn't know how to defend myself and I could die."

We wish, I thought in my head. *None of us are that lucky.*

"Uh-huh. So you don't want to be on the exploratory group that'll be finding new people? After all, those are the really cool kids, and we don't want you to feel left out."

"It's not about that. I have this bum leg from that car accident, and it's impossible for me to outrun anything that's chasing me," Bert claimed, making excuses.

"You mean, you got drunk and ran into the telephone pole, pinning your leg," a voice snickered behind me.

"Is there anyone else that feels like Bert does? I mean, if you want to go out there and fight the zombies, it would be my pleasure to show you how to do it."

Carson raised his hand from beside me, but I reached up and pulled it down.

He started to protest.

"I'll let you do the solar panel thing, but I'm still your mother, and you will not be going out there to fight those things. At least not for a few years, or when your father comes back and takes you, whichever comes first." I felt that was the end of the subject, but I should have known that an almost teenager was the beginning of trouble.

Linc would never approve of him going on a trip like that. I'd have to find a way to make him feel like we needed him at the farm. Maybe I could give him the video game system I'd borrowed from another family.

A few of the others volunteered to go, but Wade would be staying to make sure that we didn't have any problems with a coup.

The solar panels got put into place without any extra drama, and for the first time in months, I could see the lights in the sky from the town. Before the zompoc, even though Jessica's farm was out and away from the big cities, the town's lights had blended in with others in the surrounding area. Now, you could see the lights from several miles away, and when I joined everyone up in the hayloft, it was obvious that we were going to have a big problem.

If there had been electricity in other places, our town might not be as noticeable. But it was going to attract all sorts of unsavory people who wanted a town with safety.

"Blackout curtains, with only a few exceptions should keep things quiet," Tyler commented.

"Yep. They're not going to like it, but it's not like we have much choice. I'll have to alert the other towns so they can take the same precautions. It's a good thing we hadn't added the street lights back into the system yet." Linc ran a weary hand through his hair.

"Don't worry. The more things return to normal and all the cities get cleaned up, things won't seem as bad." Jessica put an arm around his waist.

"Sweetie, cleanup from this is going to last years. The world is never going to be normal. All it'll take is one person that was stuck in a closet or dies of the sickness, and we'll have a new outbreak." Linc looked at me, but he didn't say what everyone was thinking at this point.

There wasn't going to be a cure. Even if Cooper was alive, someone in our family might still die.

Without a word, I left the hayloft and went back down, settling in on the porch step to try and keep the hopelessness from overwhelming me. A tear escaped as I imagined the world my children were going to be faced with in the future.

The screen squeaked, and I turned to find Trevor coming out the door.

"Mommy?" he whispered.

"I'm right here, baby."

"Can you hold me? I'm scared of the monsters." Trevor crept closer and fixed his big eyes on me, looking for an answer.

"Yeah, come here. The monsters can't get you if I'm holding you," I reassured him, as his little body gave me comfort that I hadn't realized I needed.

"Are we going to live here forever?" Trevor snuggled into my arms, trying to get as close to me as possible.

"I hope so. I like having your Aunt Jessica around, and there are lots of fun things to do on the farm." I smiled, knowing he couldn't see it. But it made me feel better.

"Me too. I like my cousins, but I like the chickens the bestest. How come there isn't a Donald on the farm? Did he die and Aunt Jessica took over his farm?"

"What?" I asked, startled, until I remembered that he was thinking about the kid's song.

"You mean McDonald. Aunt Jessica's parents have always lived here. I think McDonald's farm is somewhere else. Maybe when you get a little older, we can go looking for Old McDonald's farm, but I think it will be just the same as Aunt Jessica's."

"Mmm…k. Then maybe we can find my friend Jon's doggie. His parents had to take it to Donald's farm so it could get better."

I swallowed the laugh that started to come out. "We just might find that doggie. You never know. Now, close your eyes and let's just sit here for a few minutes."

He settled in and I looked up at the stars, thankful that in this moment in time, my baby was still alive. I didn't need to borrow trouble, because the future had plenty of it waiting for us.

Trevor wasn't still very often. I held him until my arms were ready to collapse, and I needed to find a way to stand up without dropping him.

After a little bit of trial and error, I finally made it and laid him in my bed. It wouldn't hurt if he slept in Cooper's spot for just a little while. My eyes closed wearily, and I didn't even hear the door of Carson's room open.

It was mid-afternoon when we realized that Carson was gone, but he wasn't the only one that was missing. A group of about six teenagers had snuck out during the night and taken one of the trucks. They'd also taken a few of the guns with some ammo.

"Linc, we have to go find them," I protested.

"I understand, Trish, but they can't get far. One of the lookouts will let us know if they get to the blocked-off roads."

"What if they don't use one of the regular roads and instead take one of the dirt roads that we're not guarding? We have to find them," I yelled in frustration.

"I've already radioed the other towns, but none of the lookouts have seen them yet. We're going to do a search of the surrounding area, but remember, we could go right past them and have no clue they were in the same spot."

Jessica started to give me a hug when I spied Roxanne standing over to the side, listening intently to what was being said.

"Roxanne, do you know something about Carson?

Where he went, or if he mentioned something in the past few days?"

She started to inch back out of the kitchen, but saw that all three of us adults were watching.

Rolling her eyes and giving us a big sigh to show that her cooperation was under duress, she came into the room.

"They went to go find the liquor store that sells to teens over in the next county. They figured if they raided it now and brought back the stuff, then they could sell it to the other town's kids when they went to install their electricity." Roxanne shrugged, like we were making too big of a deal out of it.

"Was that the only place they were going?" Jessica motioned her to the chair.

"Yes. They didn't think it would take more than a day, and the adults wouldn't miss them until they were back and had hidden everything." Roxanne crossed her arms in a show of defiance. "They weren't hurting anyone or anything."

"Jessica, do you know where this place is at?" Linc apparently thought she knew, since this didn't appear to be the first time she'd heard it mentioned.

"No. They move the location every four years. The

seniors are the only ones who know where it is, and the juniors move it so that no one can snitch on it."

"Roxanne, how did you know about it when you haven't started your freshman year yet?" Jessica asked.

"Mom, come on. Everyone knows about it, we just don't know where it's at. I've been to a few parties that had alcohol there." Roxanne quickly added, "I didn't drink, but it was available."

"I'd say you're grounded, but since you can't really go anywhere, it won't mean much. I'll come up with some extra chores once we find your cousin, though," Jessica angrily threatened.

"Now I wish I'd gone with them so at least I could have had some fun before being punished," Roxanne mumbled quietly.

"She's right," Linc agreed. "She told us what was going on, and those parties were months ago."

"Stay out of it." Jessica turned her anger onto Linc. "You're not her parent, so you don't get to decide things like this. That said, I'm going to calm down before this gets crazy." Jessica turned back to Roxanne. "Is there anything else you can tell us about what direction they went in?"

"The other kids were saying it's over in the next county, toward the mountains. They didn't say where it was, and I can't believe that they invited Carson to go with them. One of the junior, or I guess the senior girls, has a crush on him."

"What? That means she's way older than he is, and…" I sputtered.

"He did tell her that he was older. Everyone thinks he's fifteen, not thirteen. When he had his birthday right after you guys got here, he told everyone he was older. I wasn't going to out him. It didn't seem fair since we were all going to die anyway," Roxanne explained.

"Oh my God. This is just getting worse. She's out there with my kid doing who knows what." I sat down in a chair, all of my anger draining because this was way more than I could take in at the moment.

"I know you ladies aren't going to like it, but guys do it all the time to impress a girl." Linc glanced at Jessica. "If you don't mind, Trish, I'll have a talk with him when he gets back and make sure he understands the ramifications of lying about his age."

"Yeah, and he's more than grounded. He's going to be doing chores until he's so tired, he can't find ways to sneak out," I groaned. "This is so much worse than if he'd done this before things went to crap. Now, the dead are after him, as well as a cougar teen."

"Hey, it's not Tina's fault. She thought he was older, and with all of the muscles he's gotten from working on the farm, she's not the only one interested in him. Even if they do it, it's not like he had ID that she could check, you know." Roxanne tried to help us understand where they were coming from.

"Roxanne, while I appreciate that you're trying to help, you're not. Even if this Tina hussy didn't know better, Carson did."

"Carson's too scared to do more than make-out with her. He's not ready for that. I'm sorry, Aunt Trish."

"I can't believe you guys are talking about this stuff already. I'm not mad at you, Roxanne. It's just really frustrating."

"He's a thirteen-year-old boy. Of course he's talking about stuff like this, and the things he's already seen since you guys got to the farm tend to make a kid grow up faster. He's smart, and won't do anything stupid, but we do need to find them before it gets dark. We'll worry about his reputation when he gets back." Linc turned and began walking out the door to go with the team trying to find the kids.

"I hope they find them." I placed my head in hands, feeling helpless.

"They will. I have faith in Linc and the others. They have a few hours before dark, and I'll bet the kids left a trail behind without knowing it," Jessica surmised, trying to comfort me.

"Actually, I was starting to feel really sorry for myself, but instead, I'm just going to give Cooper a piece of my mind when he gets back. It's his son he's left behind to languish while he 'saves the world.' To be honest, I don't see the world becoming a better place, and this superhero complex needs to be over with now." I got up and started pacing.

"Let's go outside so we can keep an eye on things while we wait for them to come back." Jessica didn't even try to talk me out of waiting, even though we both knew it would be hours before they could possibly be back, and it might be tomorrow if they had to stay someplace holed up.

"Roxanne, it's time for you to make yourself useful and keep the kids from finding out about this. Play some games out back on the swing set, then cereal for dinner so we don't burn anything because we're worried and not paying attention," Jessica ordered.

I smiled gratefully, because at this point, my mind could only focus on one thing, and that was getting Carson back safely.

It had been dark for about an hour and the kids were already in bed when lights turned up the driveway.

I squeezed Jessica's hand, because at that moment, I wanted to shout and scream at Carson for doing something so stupid. Yet, at the same time, I just wanted to hold him and cry because he was safe.

The truck doors opened and Linc, Josh, and Sam got out, but Carson didn't.

"Where is he?" I ran to the truck and frantically looked in the back seat. Empty. The truck bed was also empty.

"I'm sorry. We didn't find them, and it was pointless to continue searching in the dark with infected out there," Linc conceded.

"No! You should have kept looking!" I yelled as I started hitting the side of the truck, before collapsing to the ground, too exhausted to keep fighting.

Linc crouched down in front of me.

"We'll go back out first thing in the morning and look again. We've also kept in touch with the other blockades, and they didn't try to come through there. We're checking out all the dirt roads into the other county, but until we can get to city hall over there, we have no access to where there might be a shack or building they could be using."

"Instead of going out for more solar equipment, I've talked to a few of the other leaders, and they're going to send men to help, and we're going to work toward moving our area out farther so we can accomplish two things in one sweep. It'll put us closer to the city and keep the dead from making their way down here," Tyler informed Linc, as well as the others standing around helplessly.

"It doesn't matter. That won't find them because it took us weeks to make the kind of progress you're talking about. The closer to the city you go, the more dead you'll find." I hugged my arms around my body, keeping everything together-ish.

"We'll find them," Tyler promised.

"Don't make promises that you don't know you can keep. They could all be dead, and we would have a hard time identifying them after just a few days. I'm going to go inside now."

I had only walked a few feet when I realized that these guys had also spent a day dealing with the dead for me.

"Thank you. You guys did try and I appreciate that. Did you tell the other families?"

"I radioed Wade, and he's letting the families know that we're going to try again tomorrow." Linc nodded at the others so they could leave if they wanted.

"They needed to know. Thank you for not keeping them in the dark about it." I hurried into the house and closed the bedroom door, thankful that we'd already put the kids to bed and I'd have the room to myself.

The lock clicked, and while I was sure Jessica had a key somewhere, at least it gave me some privacy. I took the pillow from the bed and sat on the floor, holding it over my mouth to quiet the sobs that just wouldn't stop.

Numbness set in, as my body had no more energy. I had no idea when sleep took me, but I didn't remember losing consciousness.

Weeks passed with no word, and I knew that Linc hated coming back to the farm empty-handed.

The town had acknowledged that they couldn't keep

using resources to find the missing kids. Before the infected, the entire world would have been looking for them, but now that the dead were the problem, they had to assume they were also dead.

Every morning, I wanted to get up and set out by myself, but I knew that my other children didn't need to lose their father, mother, and brother. So for their sakes, I tried to put on a happy face and do things to keep our small part of the world running properly. But every night, I spent hours just looking at the stars and hoping Carson was still alive and could see them as well.

Chapter 3

Two months after the zombies hit...

Cole

When the grate closed over our heads, I knew the situation was messed up. The lights and music threw me off, and I was unsure what kind of looney bin I'd landed in when someone cut the spotlight.

"Gerald, what have we said about greeting guests with your theatrical flair?"

"I'm Lee Robinson. Sorry for the dramatics. Gerald is used to being on stage and is having a hard time without an audience. So what can we help you with?"

I frowned, wondering what these people were

playing at. "We're looking for their roommates." I nodded at Andi and Stacy, who were standing behind me. "They were supposed to be at the movie theater, but it was empty when we arrived. The girls' names are Sam and Jennifer."

"Oh, yes. We rescued them yesterday. I'm sorry you came all this way. Let me radio them and let them know you're here. Who should I say is calling?" Lee held up the radio in his hand like it was normal to greet people in the sewers, as if they'd rang the doorbell on a house.

"Um, Stacy and Andi are their roommates," I offered, exchanging a look of distrust with Darren, Stacy's boyfriend.

"Certainly. Hey, Sarah Beth? Can you have Jen and Sam come down and greet our guests please?" Lee motioned to a few old benches that were placed against the wall. "Do you want to have a seat while we wait for them?"

"No, thank you. I prefer to stand. How many people are you taking care of here?"

Lee glanced at the obvious display of weapons those in our group were holding, ready to use if necessary.

"I prefer not to say since we have no idea what your intentions really are." Lee seemed to appreciate the irony in the situation.

Andi threw a dirty look in my direction and came

out from behind me. "Look, I got a message that Sam was in danger, and we got here as quickly as we could, trying to get through all the ZITs. I just want to make sure she and her group are safe."

"They had done a wonderful job of staying out of the...what did you call them? ZITs?" Lee rubbed a hand over the stubble on his face.

"The Army named them Zombie Infected Things, or ZITs," River informed him, with her bat slung over her shoulder.

A girl that could take care of herself was something I didn't see every day. So sexy. Dammit! Focus on the suspicious leader, Cole.

"I want to make sure the girls are okay, and then we can get out of your hair."

"Nonsense. If the girls know you and say that you're safe, we'll have you stay and eat dinner with us. We just want to do a little vetting before inviting you into our secret lair. I'm sure you understand," Lee advised.

"Now who's being dramatic?" Gerald snickered.

"You know what?" I glanced around at our little group. "I think we'll just get them and start back so we don't get caught in the dark."

These guys were giving me the creeps, and it wasn't

because they wanted to vet things, either.

"We'll just let the girls decide for themselves…oh, and here they are. Jen, Sam, do you know these people?" Lee motioned to us like we were up for inspection on the auction block.

He shouldn't have even tried to speak, because Jen and Stacy raced for each other, crying, while Andi gave Sam a high five.

"I see. If you would like to come with us, we have warm food ready to be eaten." Lee just took their emotional reunions as normal, and his suspicious nature was suddenly gone.

"What makes you think we won't see your setup and take it over for ourselves?" Darren questioned.

"You could, but then you'd have to kill us in the church, and I'm pretty sure that God frowns on that."

"Are you part of a church or something?" Andi asked, puzzled.

"Sort of. If you'll follow me, I'll explain as we go." He turned and began to move at a brisk pace.

"Our church's family center is considered a Red Cross station when there is a disaster, but we also help house the homeless when there is an imminent weather threat. We were setup for the overflow from the hospitals and ready as a first triage area where the super sick could be sent to the ER. Thankfully, things got crazy before the sick arrived, or we would have had a mess on our hands.

"I was one of the extra staff, but my brother was the associate pastor. He didn't make it that first week, before we knew what was going on. I was able to get my nieces and bring them back here for safety." Lee's face held a hint of sadness, but he continued past the pain. "We're also a food pantry, so there were quite a few supplies here, but not many members actually showed up when things went from bad to worse."

The sewer ended at a door that could be sealed up to keep the water or other things from getting inside. It was already open, and a guard was standing outside with a gun.

At least they weren't completely stupid about this, I thought as we walked inside with our weapons. Were guns allowed in church?

A short hallway walk and we were in the basement, guarded by another person on lookout. It wasn't a complete setup like the army would have done, but at least they were giving it a try.

"The ZITs, as you called them, made it almost impossible to move between the larger and more secure church building, and the showers over in the family building. I checked for several ideas and ran across the plans from the early days of the church, back when prohibition was in place."

"You've got to be shitting us? The church was holding onto a secret speakeasy? From those days? I thought churches were against alcohol." Darren glanced at me, and I shrugged.

"I uncovered the plans hidden in one of the old closets. We literally took the place apart to fortify it and to find anything that could be useful. I'd remembered some stories from my days up in Bethel about the moonshine, and how the town first got built by my ancestors," Lee informs us.

"Not Bethel, up in the mountains where they kidnap their women to bring fresh blood to the area? My family is over on Jackson Mountain, about a two-day trek as the crow flies." I suddenly felt much better about the man in front of me knowing he was a local.

"Hey, we're practically relatives. We might even have some distant relatives as well. Anyway, things haven't progressed much through the years as far as technology, but once in a while, some of us will want to get off the mountain, which is what happened to my brother and I. Our parents died of something that came through about fifteen years ago, and instead of staying up there, we decided to come down here and see if we could make it."

Lee's acceptance of death made a lot more sense now, knowing that he came from the sturdy mountain men. For most of those that lived in the mountains, death was a lot more commonplace as part of the circle of life.

"So these plans for the underground system were drawn out and connected to a couple of places in the downtown area. They would have one speakeasy open and deliver stuff to the church's stables or carriage house, as it was renamed later, across the street. No one even looked at deliveries to a church, and they were taken to the speakeasy that was running that week. When they built the family center, they covered over the door, and it took some work trying to get it opened up. This also allowed us a way to move around without drawing the dead after us, or bringing them to the church."

"That's quite the setup, which means you have a lot of people here and spread out through town," I muttered, knowing why he was so confident that we wouldn't take over their operation.

"It sounds like you have it all figured out, but I think the military had the right idea about using the college campuses. I guess either way could work," River commented, looking things over as we walked.

"You're with the military? Do they have extra ammo that we could use to help clear areas out?" Lee actually seemed excited at the prospect of help from people with guns.

"Retired military," Darren tersely answered.

"Or mostly just experienced in ZIT killing. No guns are necessary for taking down those things when there aren't that many of them." River grinned as she patted her bloodstained bat.

"Well, we didn't have an armory around here, and have only found a few guns, but we could always use more for when the ZITs get bottled up in a herd." Lee finally opened a door leading to newly built steps up to the surface level.

"Welcome to the Church Against Zombies," Gerald boomed to the people sitting around the gymnasium.

His announcement didn't even faze the people sitting around on cots.

"This way to the kitchen. We're having stew this evening." Gerald waved to an open hallway and a kitchen area.

"Jen, do you and Sam want to stay here, or should we head out?" Stacy asked, giving them the option to warn us of anything that could be harmful.

"Do you have somewhere that has hot food?" Sam looked over at Stacy without letting go of Andi's arm.

"Not for tonight," she responded.

"Then I vote we stay here. I haven't had much besides mounds of popcorn for a while now. It sounds good at first, but when it's all you have to eat, it gets old fast." Sam pulled Andi closer, if that was even possible.

"It's decided then. Come, and we will answer any of the questions I know you still have for us." Lee led us, making sure to take the first bowl so that we would know it was safe to eat.

The cooks in the kitchen reminded me of the ladies that were always buzzing around whenever we had a family gathering. If any of us had suggested that we help, they would have been greatly offended. Besides, it was the best use of their skills, because these ladies would likely fall over if they attempted to kill a zombie.

"Evening, ladies," I greeted them with a smile. Lots of people were reassured with a simple smile, even though I was a big guy. I tried not to scare people. "Sure smells delicious."

The others followed my lead and took the rations we were handed.

It didn't take Andi long to ask the question I knew she'd been holding back. I was one of the few that knew she had a crush on Sam's older brother, Sean.

"Where's your family, Sam? Are they still at your house?"

Sam burst into tears, which Andi took in stride by placing a hand on her shoulder.

"I think so. Sean was supposed to be coming home from his job when I left for the movies. The phones weren't working when we got done, and I thought we were going to die in that theater." She moaned between sobs. "It was horrible. Two of the others I was with ran toward the employee only doors and I followed them. We could see the parking lot and people were eating people, so we couldn't go out there."

"Sam, back to Sean and your family. Have you had any contact with them since this started?" Andi snapped her fingers in front of Sam to get her attention.

"Someone had a computer and that was how I was messaging you. I was able to send Sean an email as well. They were alive that first week, but I haven't heard anything since then," Sam sniffled.

Andi turned her attention to Jennifer. "Anything from your mom or dad's houses to let us know if they survived?"

Jennifer shook her head. "No, they don't have anything but cell phones, and I never thought I would need their email addresses."

"Lee, I'm guessing since you just found these guys yesterday that you haven't tried to make a rescue attempt yet?" Andi seemed to be taking charge, and I wasn't about to stop my cousin from accomplishing what I was thinking.

"Those we rescued were distressed, and the only thing they've been able to do is get clean, eat, and rest for the first night since the zompoc started," Lee informed her.

"Zompoc? You do realize that this isn't a video game, right?" I might have known where he was from, but that didn't mean I wasn't going to hassle him when I could.

"I'm well aware that this isn't a game. I watched my brother die from this illness, but there isn't really anything else to call it except the Zombie Apocalypse. If this isn't one, then I'd hate to see the real thing happen to us." Lee's voice held the anguish of someone who'd seen death up close and personal.

"Fair enough. Do you have any problems with us going out to see if we can find their families?" I casually leaned my gun against the table next to my chair.

"After dinner, I can take you to the office and show

you the map that's on the wall there. We're marking off areas we've been to and that are clear for the moment. You may find quite a few survivors, and we would be glad to welcome them here or see if we can take supplies to them if they're somewhere they feel safe." Lee paused to take a few bites of the warm stew. "A few of the others who were with them may have families in the same area. We just hadn't had a moment since we got them back to get into it."

"All right. We just need to send a message back to Jackson Mountain because we left a little abruptly this morning. I don't see why we can't find a way to work together for a little while and get a few areas cleared out before we head back," I acknowledged, picking up my spoon.

Everyone was enjoying their food, so I decided that if it was a quick acting poison, we should be past that point since no one had started choking or having any reactions.

It was good, but that wasn't really a surprise, as the church ladies were the ones doing the cooking. There was nothing like a good church potluck to realize that the cooks were gifted and very few dishes ever went in the trash.

Dinner was over, and Darren, River, and I followed Lee to the office, which held a map with pins all over it.

"Lee, do you have any kind of plan on how to clean things up and make things livable again?" I asked, crossing behind the desk to survey the map.

"We've only been up and running for about two weeks, and in that time, we cleared out the area around the courthouse. The businesses have taken a little longer simply because we were taking anything that could be used and carting it back to the church."

I noted the green highlighted area in a good two-mile circle around the church, and then a broader yellow circle.

"How far do the tunnels go? Those that have clear access, do they only go to the street or are they in to each building?" Darren inquired from behind me.

"Some of the old entries were easy to open, but we go up through that building and bring stuff from the neighboring stores. Those are the buildings that we've put guards in to make sure we're not overrun with unfriendly humans or the infected dead. Most of our group are too young or too old to be out there fighting, but they can move the stuff through the tunnels and back to the church once the supplies are in the secure building."

I nod in agreement. It's what I would have done with the fragile people around.

"Are your fighters military or just self-trained after the zompoc hit?" River stood in the doorway, away from the different amounts of testosterone filling the room.

"Actually, we have a few veterans that had been homeless. They were excited to have something useful to do, and they are more prepared for killing the dead than most of the church members were." Lee grinned ruefully.

"Let's face it, churches aren't considered the friendliest of places toward those who kill people for a living."

"Ha! You can say that again. They certainly want to instill the peaceful road to Jesus. At least the country churches don't have a problem with guns being used for hunting." Darren laughed at the idea.

"Trained fighters then. How many are we looking at? Twenty? Thirty? Five?" River brought the conversation back to the details. "I think our group would be able to go out and clear things out, but we might need to take a few of yours so we don't bring back things that wouldn't be useful in the near future."

Lee inhaled and gave us a careful glance before

answering the question. "I'm putting a lot of trust in you three. In fact, the safety of the people I love most will be compromised if my gut feeling is wrong." He sighed. "We have ten that can fight and clear things out. We've been rotating those in two groups of five—one to go out, and the other group to teach the teens and those strong enough how to take the infected out.

"We can't survive with the few we have if another group decides they want what we have. I'm one of the first to bring people in that need help, but I also have to think of the group, and that makes the decisions more difficult." Lee sank into the chair at the desk. "I just hope that your group can help us."

"If we follow the same procedures that the military did with the colleges and get things setup, we should be able to find more people that have survived, as well as supplies to last until things get up and running again." River spoke confidently, acting like she had a say in how things would be run.

"Sweetie, I believe that will be up to the leaders in each group, and I think those spots are filled with military guys."

A loud snicker made me turn to see what was the matter with Darren. "What's gives?"

"Oh, nothing. You're just digging yourself into a hole that you may not be able to get out of with River." Darren smirked at me. "But you'll find that out for yourself if you keep this up."

"She's right, you know." Lee raised his head from the back of the chair. "It makes the most sense to work with people who are already familiar with the area."

"River, will Stacy be wanting to go out with us?" Darren grinned because he knew asking beforehand would go better.

"She wasn't a fan of the ZITs, but there was also Dillon to think about, and it made her more cautious. I don't see her wanting to leave your side after you guys just got back together, though, so I'm going to say that she'll want to join us."

"Well, she's not here by his side right now, so maybe their love isn't as secure as you think, pumpkin." I calmly add fuel to the fire, feeling River's angry gaze on me.

"Ignore the heartless one in the room, River." Darren tried to catch my eye and warn me to back down, but that wasn't going to happen.

"I suggest that you all get rested up and meet the other teams. They all come in after dark, and we swap out those on lookout duty." Lee rose from the chair, but stopped when I didn't immediately move from my spot in front of the map.

"Those that were out killing infected will rest tomorrow, and our B team will go with your team."

"Guess we just took your A team spot." I confidently headed to the door, expecting Darren and Lee to follow me back out to the eating area.

River's small, five-foot frame was blocking my way out. Twirling the ends of her blue-green hair, she lifted her big brown eyes up at me.

"Oh, I'm sorry, were you just going to plow on through here and take charge? Finally, someone who knows how to lead. Oh, please be my hero?" She fluttered her eyelashes.

"Huh?" I stopped mid-stride, confused because I was missing something vital. "I'm your hero?"

Her finger hit the middle of my chest and pushed me back, catching me off-guard.

"No, jackass, and you won't be anyone's if you come in here and take over. Let Lee through and he can get everyone on board."

"But he isn't military—" I started to protest when she spoke over me.

"And it's a good thing we have the military to wipe our asses, because I certainly wouldn't know where to find mine if they didn't give me lots of directions. You're going to learn to play with others, and taking over is not the way to make new friends. Let's start with please, will you introduce us to your A team?" River grinned over my shoulder at Darren and Lee.

If Darren had anything to do with this little spitfire standing up to me, I would just have to pull rank.

"What was I thinking? I should have asked your permission to proceed, General River. I mean, you've been giving orders like one. I'm sure they have crowns here for when a princess graduates to the commanding officer or something."

Her entire face turned red, but instead of saying something smart, she shoved me back and pulled the door behind her so that I was suddenly standing there with a closed door in my face.

"What the hell?" I reached to grab the knob, but Darren moved around me.

"Dude, get out of my way. I'm going to show her who's the boss around here."

"Hey, I know she's getting under your skin, but you can't let her do that to you. I've spent the last two days with her, and she's as good as she's claiming. She kept the campus clear and the military had her as the liaison between the civilians they brought in. That's not someone you want to get on your bad side. Plus, I'm pretty sure that Andi, Sam, Stacy, and Jennifer aren't going to be helpful in this instance. It happens to all of us at some point."

"Did the infection get to your brain? I have no idea what you're talking about."

Lee exchanged a smirk with Darren.

"He's got it bad."

"Yep, he sure does."

"Seriously, was there a memo that I missed?" My temper was about to get the best of me.

"It's always the strong ones that fight it the most." Darren clapped me on the back, but I shrugged his hand off.

"Sparks have been flying around you and River since you walked into the tunnel downstairs. You're in love," Lee wisely added.

"I just met the vixen. The only sparks that are going to fly around here are when her head explodes because I'm right," I announced with indignation.

"Sure. You tell yourself whatever makes you feel better, but she's gotten under your skin because she didn't just bat her eyes and fall for your charms," Lee conceded.

"Although, she did flutter her lashes at him a minute ago, but I think that was just to lull him into complacency and make fun of him. Come on, we'd better get out there before she stages a coup and has all of Lee's people following her merry tune."

I followed the other two out of the office, wondering if her not falling for my charms was the reason I was turned on when she stood up to me. This could turn out more interesting than I'd thought when I left the Mountain with Andi earlier this morning.

Chapter 4

Unhappy about staying for the night, I managed to catch a few hours of sleep, rotating with Darren. It was a long night, and every time I'd start to relax, I'd see River's devilish grin.

Just as the sun started to hit the sky, I was up and wandering around the church to see if we'd missed anything.

The smell of coffee hit my nose as I came up through the tunnel connecting the large church building with the eating area.

Lee was putting a fresh pot of loose coffee to perk as he pulled the already full one onto the hot plate.

"I'm curious. How is it that you have electricity and fresh coffee? It's not like there's been anyone to keep the plants running over the past two months."

Startled, Lee almost dropped the hot coffee when I spoke.

He placed a hand over his heart. I didn't believe I'd scared him at all. I was pretty sure that he was just leading all of us on until we let our guard down.

"We have some generators in the basement for during the winter in case the power goes out." He held up an empty cup for me to use. "The coffee? Well, we got lucky, or should I say *blessed* on that one. We found the coffee shop empty and carted all the extras back here. I'm still not used to being the shepherd of a flock. That was more my brother's job before he passed."

Nodding my head, I just listened to him ramble and walked farther into the kitchen to pour me a cup of the delicious coffee.

"What were you before that?" I might not have many weaknesses, but caffeine was one of the few addictions I allowed myself.

"Me? I was one of those that attended church on Christmas and Easter, but I didn't mind helping when he needed something done around here for the homeless."

"That didn't really answer my question. What did you do for work before the ZITs showed up?"

"Building contractor, which is why I let them open

up the doors to the tunnels. We didn't want the walls to fall down around us, but I made sure that we did it safely."

"Hmm," I mumbled noncommittally.

"Everyone has had to adjust and do things that we didn't think were possible only a few short weeks ago. Leader wasn't something I wanted to do or ever planned on before all this, but I just couldn't leave these people in the situation they were in when I got here with the girls."

"Girls?" This was getting more suspicious by the minute.

"Yeah, my nieces, Charity and Hope. People were trying to come in here, and they had no way to defend themselves against the infected. The glass had been busted out, and we were able to walk inside easily. I grew up hunting, so while I'm not a great shot, I was able to kill the ones hanging out before letting everyone out of the room they were trapped in."

"Now I get it. You saved them, and they follow you blindly anywhere you lead." I took a sip of the coffee.

Tough guys would have tried to drink it down and prove how brave they were, but I preferred the common sense approach to let it cool off slightly before downing it.

"What? Oh, no. I just happened to be in the right place at the right time. Most of the members who were here wouldn't make it out there on their own. Together we're stronger." He sounded like he was trying to convince himself of that.

Refilling the cup, I didn't make any other comments, since several of the older ladies were coming in to start making breakfast. It was the perfect time to sneak away, because while this Lee guy might not have planned to be the hero, he could certainly sell anything if he talked to you long enough.

Our group had collected in the basement to move out to the manhole we'd come down in and back to our vehicles. They had gas in them, and it wouldn't take too long to have them ready to leave versus the group's vehicles that had been beaten up trying to clear out the area.

"River will you take the A team and go with Jennifer to see if her family is alive." A peace offering seemed like a good idea, especially since I had an ace up my sleeve.

"Sure." She eyed me suspiciously. "Now you want me to lead a group?"

"No better time than now to find out if you can handle it. Darren speaks highly of your skills, so let's see what you've got."

"Where are you going to be?"

"Right here behind you, watching your six." I held both hands out in front of me in surrender.

"Load up then. And Darren, we'll keep in contact with you as we get close to the area before we split off." She slung the bat over her shoulder and climbed into the seat of the reinforced jeep.

It wasn't until I pulled open the passenger door that she realized I would be riding with her.

"Ah, hell no. Get out." She pointed to the other vehicle that pulled away at that moment.

"Guess you're stuck with me now." I tried to hide my smirk so that I didn't cause her to explode.

With a dramatic huff, she put the jeep in gear. "Whatever."

The roads were littered with abandoned vehicles, and in a few spots, we had to get out and push some over to make a path. A few of Lee's guys would help keep watch while one of the smaller girls would put the car into neutral so that we could use the jeep to get it rolling.

After the first two, River opened up her door and

started to get down.

"Where are you going?" I demanded.

"Not that it's any of your business, but there are quite a few ZITs moving this way since we've been making noise, and if we use any more bullets, the group over in that shopping center will have us for lunch." She tapped the bat. "This baby is as silent as they come."

The next thing I knew, Jennifer was climbing up into the jeep, and River was proving why she'd been on a softball scholarship before the zompoc hit.

It was a thing of beauty to watch until I realized that I could be out there with her instead of letting Darren have all the fun.

I picked up a metal pole that was a little longer than a bat.

It was perfect.

A growl behind me had me turning to swing before I'd even gotten a chance to test it, but what could be better than testing it on the real thing?

The next ZIT's head almost separated from its neck with the force of my frustration behind the swing. While I still liked having my gun as a backup, I could get used to hitting for the fences and taking these things out one by one. It was one way to stay in shape.

River waved frantically at the jeep, and Jennifer revved the engine up as she crept forward, until she was touching the bumper of the cars blocking the road.

Once free of the bottleneck, a group of infected swarmed toward us, drawing those that had been lagging behind closer to where we'd taken a stand.

With several of us working to take out the ZITs, the vehicles were able to creep forward a little at a time. What would have normally taken about twenty minutes took closer to four hours, and we were almost to the neighborhood where Jennifer's parents lived.

Even during the panic, the cars were stacked up on the off-ramp in lines, with only a small space to squeeze through to make it on to the streets.

It was easier to maneuver around the abandoned cars since most people had pulled over before leaving their vehicles. At some point, a group would have to bring a pump out here and empty all the cars of gas. No point in having a resource go to waste.

The wandering dead were fewer as we reached the entrance to their subdivision, and the bricked walls surrounding the housing area.

Those of us that had been clearing the highway had hopped into the back of the trucks until we pulled up in front of a modest home.

I jumped to the ground, glancing around to see if there were any signs of life.

"Jennifer, stay back, and once we've gone through the house, we'll let you come in and get your clothes, or whatever we can take with us. The rest of you split up and make sure this side of the street is empty," River ordered efficiently.

"I'll come with you," Jennifer tried to protest, until I caught her in a hug.

"Sweetie, if they're alive, then you'll be right here to greet them, but no one should have to see their family dead or have to put them down like that."

Everyone else moved away from us, and I decided to stay right there, because if left by herself, Jennifer was going to do something stupid.

"We good to go?" River asked.

I nodded and stood next to Jennifer as they unlocked the door.

"Anyone home? Mrs. Hill, are you in there?" River called out.

Nothing came to the door, so she and the two others behind her moved inside.

It was really quiet for a few minutes, then a crash

had me tightening my grip around Jennifer.

"What was that? Is she hurt?" Jennifer started crying. "I can't take it." She buried her face in my shoulder, sobbing harder, drenching my shirt.

Seconds later, the team emerged empty-handed.

"No one's inside," River quietly announced. "Is there anywhere she would go?"

"Is her car there?" Jennifer took off running for the house.

"Did you clear the closets as well?"

"Yes, I did, sir." River saluted me before following her inside so they could load up anything the church could use.

Frustrated that River was still being sassy, I walked to where the other group was opening the garage of the house three doors down.

A spotless pickup truck was sitting inside, and they were carrying laundry baskets full of pantry items out to the bed of the truck.

I was beginning to feel like a third wheel, until I heard growls starting to grow in volume.

Everyone else was occupied, so I went to the corner of the block and discovered a herd of dead moving in our direction. While we'd been really quiet, it hadn't been quiet enough.

I took off at a run and waved to the group filling the truck. "Make that the last load. There's a group headed our way."

But I didn't stop until I was inside with River.

"What's wrong?" she questioned seriously.

"There's a herd about three blocks away and they're moving fast. We need to get out of the housing area now."

"Let's go. Everyone out, now!" River urged, counting heads as they left with whatever they were carrying out to the trucks.

"Jennifer, we have to leave now."

River started to go back, but I pushed past her into the house.

Jennifer was standing in the hallway, looking at the pictures on the walls.

"Come on." I grabbed at her arm, only to have her turn back toward the bedroom.

She came back lugging a large suitcase behind her.

I shook my head. Trying to pry clothes from a woman was like asking them to leave part of themselves behind.

"Go, I've got it. Hurry!"

The handle on the suitcase was broken, and it had to

be pushed to the front door.

River had started up the truck and turned around, facing out by the time I got it to the tailgate. One of the church guys, Wayne, hopped down to help me lift it into the truck.

I jumped in and pulled it closed after me. River sped away quickly, catching up to the other vehicles waiting for us at the end of the street.

We'd made it out in the nick of time, because the first of the infected were in Jennifer's front yard.

We were going to have to set some ground rules for the next few stops, and I would have to help tell Darren's group the same thing when we all got back this evening.

Jennifer's dad's house was two major streets down from where we'd ended up. It was highly unlikely that anyone was alive in that subdivision.

Unlike the last neighborhood, this one seemed eerie, like there were eyes watching us.

As everyone piled out of the vehicles, I motioned them all to gather around.

"We almost got screwed over last time. We can't afford to make mistakes or it'll mean going home with fewer people. If it means getting the supplies or living, leave it. Nothing is worth your life." I gave Jennifer a pointed look. She had the common sense to look ashamed.

"From now on, we'll have someone on lookout at the end of each street in a vehicle, with another person who can run inside and warn people. There may be a few stragglers that pop up, but we don't want to get pinned in by one of those large groups that we won't be able to outrun."

Proud of my speech, I was taken off-guard when a gunshot rang out inches from where I was standing.

I ducked and found the shooter two doors down, peering out from a window in the house.

Raising my hands in the air, I started to approach.

"Cole, what are you doing?" River ground out from the front of the truck.

"I'm gonna go get us a few recruits."

"Cocky idiot." Her words lingered as I moved toward the house where the shot had come from.

A man showed up on the porch, holding his weapon in front of him in such a way that I knew he had never been taught gun safety.

"We're just looking for Al Hill. We've got his daughter Jennifer with us, and we're trying to find out if he's still alive."

"I don't want nothin' to do with you, but if Al's still alive, he'd probably be hiding in his shed."

I was close enough to see that the unkempt gentleman was shaking.

"We're from the First Church downtown. I'm not much on religion myself, but they have hot showers and coffee. We could always use someone else to help with watch duty. If you've got anyone else with you that you want to bring, it would be okay with our group." I moved closer, never taking my eyes off his finger until he pointed the gun to the ground.

"Church? We've been taking care of our own and haven't seen any group that wasn't looking to ransack our houses. We've managed to take care of ourselves just fine so far."

"Really? Well, I guess we'll just be checking on Jennifer's dad and see if any of your neighbors feel the same way." I turned back toward the group when he spoke again.

"I guess it wouldn't hurt to go someplace that had electricity."

"Great," I enthusiastically announced. "Maybe you can help us knock on the right doors so we don't leave anybody behind?"

"Sure, sure. There are the four houses here, and then one on the back side. We've pretty much been through the area and cleaned out all the houses of anything that was edible," he admitted, rubbing his beard. "I'm Ed, by the way."

I held out my hand. "Cole Jackson, nice to meet you."

A squeal brought my attention over to the group where Jennifer was jumping up and down between a man and woman.

"That would be Al and his ex-wife, Nancy. I guess your girl found her parents. I'll just grab a few things and meet you outside in a minute." Ed coughed and turned back to his house.

Crap! He's sick, and I'm going to bring him back to the others, but it could just be a cold. Maybe I'm overreacting.

"Hey, Ed is going to come with us." I introduced the neighbor as we got a little closer.

"You must be Jennifer's parents. Good to see you all in one piece. Ed here was telling me that you've searched this area pretty well. We're going to knock on a few of the doors and get ready to head out, if no one has any objections?" I glanced around at the group, and other than River, no one even seemed to care that I'd taken charge.

"If you two could pack a quick bag of clothes, we can make it back to the church before dark hits and get you fixed up with some food." I smiled at the reunited family.

"Does anyone have any extra ammo or food that needs to be taken with us?" I asked as the other neighbors gathered around, preparing to leave.

"No. I used the last round on warning you." Ed grinned sheepishly. "We've been out of food for a few days now, and were about to draw numbers as to who we should eat first."

The horror in my thoughts must have shown on my face, because Al chuckled. "We weren't gonna eat anyone. It just meant that we were gonna have to leave the neighborhood to scavenge some more. Nancy's house still has food, but I didn't want to travel that far over with only the two of us. We managed to take out those that got sick and died. If you get around more than one or two of those things, you can be overwhelmed really fast."

"Well, are we missing anyone?"

River shook her head no, as did Ed.

"Let's get on with it then."

The trip back was much easier because we were going against the traffic back through the path that we'd already cleared. While it was a faster trip, the open spaces made it where the ZITs could move more freely and group up easier.

I just hoped that the other group had had as happy of an ending as we had.

Chapter 5

Andi

I was shocked when Cole went with the other group, until I realized that he was going to follow River around like a little puppy trying to protect someone that clearly didn't need it.

Darren was a wonderful substitute with his military training, and I knew that if we had a chance of finding Sam's family, he would be the reason.

While I love my friend Sam, she wasn't the sort to hold up under pressure, and I'd tried to convince her all evening that she wouldn't want to go with us, that it was a gory, violent mess out there. I wasn't far behind her in the hating anything that consisted of exercise, but she had always been protected from everything by her family.

She was going to have to get a thicker skin in this new world of the zompoc. At least my family had always made sure that I was at least trained in self-defense, even if they never really let me practice it. Maybe things were changing—not that I really wanted to live out the world of video games on the streets of a real city.

Sean had moved out of his parents' house a few years ago, but still managed to hit them up for laundry and to raid the refrigerator.

Our group had decided to stay off the highways and take the back streets, hoping that if we found something the group could use, we could stop on the way back if we had enough daylight left.

The infected were out here and there, but the groups were a little harder to ignore, and seemed to congregate in the shopping areas, which would have the best supplies.

Sam's house was in the older part of town, with many of the homes needing to be remodeled on one of those TV fixer-upper shows.

"Tony, take a few of the guys, and keep a lookout for any signs of life while we see if Sam's family is here."

He aimed his weapon at the door and I turned the knob.

The sight that greeted us was horrible, and the smell

was worse. There wasn't anything alive in this house, but for Sam's sake, we went ahead and checked.

I slid my T-shirt over my nose, but all that did was make me smell how sweaty and nervous I was at the thought of what we were going to find in the house.

The long hallway might have been a good idea at some point, but it simply heightened my fear as I crept into the living room, with Darren at my back.

Two people were sitting on the couch with their heads having bled out from the wounds inflicted by a gunshot. I wasn't an expert, but it looked like they had been covered before someone had put them out of their misery.

"Are those Sam's parents?" Darren asked, looking into the kitchen before he motioned me to the hall leading to the bathroom.

"Yeah, it looks like Sean might've been here at some point. I just hope we don't find him up there. It would be really weird to stay here with the dead bodies while you were still alive."

"Sounds like a movie, but it is kind of creepy. All this is enough to make normal people go a little crazy, so be prepared for anything, okay?" He gently tried to get me ready for whatever else we found.

The upstairs was empty, but when we looked in the

kitchen to see if there were any supplies, they were all gone.

"Can you think of anywhere else he might have gone?"

"He'll have gone back to the apartment he shared with the other guys, but before we head over there, I'm going to grab all the toilet paper and shampoo they have."

"That's brilliant. I wouldn't have ever thought we needed to get supplies from all over the house. I'd have just gotten the kitchen and food stuff."

Not finding Sean meant he could still be alive out there. Although, the thought of trying to tell him and Sam that their parents hadn't made it, almost made me want to hold off on finding him. I couldn't come back to Sam completely empty-handed, though.

"So how long have you liked this Sean guy?" Darren asked, holding a laundry basket full of soap, shampoo, and deodorant.

"Huh? I never said I liked Sean. I mean, he's like a brother, and he's Sam's brother." I really hoped that I wasn't blushing.

Ugh! This is why I hate talking to real people. When it was through my screen, I could come off sounding funny or witty. In real life, there was no way to hide from prying eyes, always trying to figure me out.

"It's pretty obvious, and while I'm sure that you're concerned for Sam's family, he's the main reason you made the trip from Jackson Mountain. The question is, does he know that you have a crush on him?" Darren had both of his hands full, but still paused on the porch to check our surroundings before walking toward the truck.

"I've liked him for years, yet there was always the fact that I was Sam's friend, and girls don't really exist in the gamer world."

"Now that's not true. Girls are all throughout the geek world. I mean, having hot geeky girls is the 'in' thing."

"In one way you're so right, but even though the guys have let us into their world and are pretty accepting, they don't come out of their caves long enough to meet us. They're so scared we're going to bite that they act like we don't exist. If you're just one of the guys, then they don't have to face the fact you might like them or reject them. They can't deal with it either way."

"You seem pretty adjusted."

"Thanks, but that's just because I have one of those very nosy families that don't take no for an answer, and it's better to come out of hiding and join in so they'll leave you alone."

We stood lookout until the others brought back all that they could carry.

"So Sam's parents were in there, but not her brother. Andi knows where the guy lives, and there isn't any point in hanging around here. It's also closer to that store we found that might have food in it. Anyone object with adding Sean's place to the list?"

I let out a sigh of relief. Maybe this wouldn't be a wasted trip, and we could find someone alive.

There was a large group of dead people blocking the entrance to their apartment complex, but Darren slowly pulled out in front of the herd, leading them down ten blocks. Our group sped up, leaving them farther behind, but heading in a forward direction while we doubled back.

I'd seen a strange flag on the top of one of the apartments, but couldn't tell what it said.

The gate blocking the back entrance was closed, but one of the guys from the church pulled it open manually, leaving it open behind us.

"It's building E toward the front. I think he's on the second floor, but I could be wrong. I've only been here twice."

Darren patted my arm. "Don't worry. If he's here and alive, we'll find him."

The group split up into teams of two, but only after Darren had given them a new set of instructions. "Collect all toiletries, as well as kitchen items. Batteries and any type of guns or ammo. If you're not sure, then ask either Tony or I, and we'll let you know if it's something we can use."

A whistle pierced the air before we could start our canvas.

I placed a hand over my eyes so that I could look up where the sound was coming from.

"Hey, we can come down and open the door. Don't break it down. Give us five minutes," a voice from above called down.

I looked around to make sure that we hadn't alerted any of the undead, and hoped that Sean was one of the ones who were still alive.

The door flew open and our group was tackled by about ten college guys and a few other people.

They were so excited to see people that they were

hugging everyone. I was suddenly engulfed in a strong embrace.

"Andi? God, I'm glad to see you. Is Sam with you?" Sean released me just a little bit, but didn't let go of me fully.

"She's at the church," I muttered quietly, pushing back so that I could look at his face.

"Sean, your parents...they're gone."

He didn't seem to notice that I'd pushed him away, but he moved in closer, giving me another hug. "I know. I found them on the second day and came back here since I had no idea where Sam was at."

"I'm so sorry." I wiped a tear away, and for once, actually missed my dad and stepmom.

"It'll be okay. At least I know they're not out there eating other people. We'll find a way to tell Sam together," he promised, keeping an arm around me as we stood waiting for Darren to tell us what to do next.

"You guys were an unexpected find, so we're going to need to find a few more vehicles that we can get running to help transport everyone over to the church. Collect everything, but only take a small amount of clothes. We don't have room for any keepsakes. If things settle down in a few weeks, there's no reason that we can't come back here and get more stuff."

"Hey, you need to come with me and help me pack up the electronics." Sean grabbed my hand and pulled me after him, toward the stairs.

"Sean, we don't have enough electricity to run a game system or laptop at the church. They have only the important things, like the refrigerators going."

"No problem. I've got a small solar powered energy cube. It's the only thing that's kept us sane when we thought the rest of the world was dead." Sean grinned in excitement.

"Oh, well, in that case, lead the way." I dropped his hand, unsure if he knew the signals he was sending my direction.

"It's not very big, and can only run a few things at a time, but I think if we can scavenge at a building supply store, the guys and I could setup a system that'll help us regenerate the energy we use."

"We've hit the brainlode with you guys and all of your degrees. The only question is, can you actually do something with all you've learned or is it all just talk?" I couldn't help teasing him as we made it to the roof through the small access hole.

It was covered in wires crisscrossing everywhere,

but Sean walked straight over to the small panel facing the sun.

He picked up a baby monitor. "Hey, Finn, let everyone know I'm about to disconnect the lights so I can bring it with me."

Seeing me standing there watching, must have made him realize how silly he looked.

He had on normal college guy comfortable clothes, including socks with his sandals, but if I didn't know him so well, he would have looked a little crazy.

"You think we've gone insane, don't you?" He started unhooking wires and rolling them into a backpack.

I shook my head, trying to hold back a giggle. "Where do you want me to start?"

"We're going to need everything on the left side there, and I'll take the right."

"Were you guys just planning to stay up here for the rest of your lives?"

"Nah. We went hunting every few days for supplies, and to help keep the population thinned out around here."

He walked over, standing close behind me. "See the rooftop over there? We have plants growing, and our own irrigation system from the rain. Each one of the buildings has a fresh rainwater tub, so when the plumbing quit working, we rigged it up. The sewers keep going as long as you have something to flush it with."

"I'm sure the people at the church will be glad to have you setup something like this for them."

"Oh, I'm coming back here after I see Sam. We've got a pretty good crop going up here, and it's fresh food. But if we don't watch over it, the plants will die." Sean leaned in close and whispered, "Plus, I have a few 'herb' plants for recreational purposes."

"What! No way. Sean, that's illegal." I turned around and found my shock seep away when I was only inches from my crush.

"Andi, really? Do you see the police or DEA hanging out to stop us from growing our pot? The world has gone to crap, and if this is one way to relax, then I'm all for it."

"It's so dangerous." I placed a hand on his chest, feeling his heartbeat. "If you're relaxed, then you won't hear the infected because you're not paying attention."

He placed a kiss on my forehead to pacify me, before moving to gather up the other stuff.

I'd known Sean's group smoked on occasion, but I'd never been around when they were doing it. In a sense, I could see where he was coming from, but I hadn't ever done that at school because of my dad and cousins always breathing down my neck.

"You do have a point. Maybe when it's safe, you could let me try it for the first time."

"Ah, an herb virgin. I guarantee that the guys and I can pop that cherry for you, and what better place to do it from? A church!"

I blushed. "You don't have to be sacrilegious about it. What if lightning strikes?"

Sean started to laugh, until he saw that I was serious.

"Look, I don't know about much in the way of a god or religion, but if 'God' created everything, then he also made the herb for man to use or consume. Pretty sure he's got his hands full right now with the sudden influx of people waiting to be vetted for heaven." He scratched at his chin. "Although, I've never heard of having to be vetted for hell. I might have to ask the preacher that question."

"All set to cut the power." Finn's voice came over the baby monitor.

"Right. Almost done here. We should be down in five." Sean zipped up the backpack and went over to the solar panel, unplugging it from the wires running down the side of the apartment building.

He gently wrapped it in a blanket before putting it in his large duffle bag.

"I'm going to have you go down the ladder, and then I'll hand the bags to you so that they don't get jarred or broken."

I glanced down at the group loading up into the trucks as I went to descend into the dark hallway.

The hatch in the ceiling was the only source of light, and I began to get nervous while I waited for Sean to hand down the bags.

"Sean, can you hurry up please?" I called softly.

Instead of an answer, all the light was blocked out as the bag filled the opening.

Not wanting to panic, I counted as I inhaled. Reaching up, grabbed at the bag.

We hadn't thought this through, because I wasn't tall enough to reach the bag without being on the stairs.

A hand reached past me and I screamed.

"Andi, are you okay?" Sean pulled the bag back, trying to see me.

"Finn, quit playing around and help me get this stuff down."

I stood back against the wall, holding a hand over my still thundering heart.

"I thought I was dead there for a second," I grumbled as Finn set one bag down and reached for the second one.

"That was the point, Cherry."

"Sorry. I'm Andi."

"I know, but since we're going to pop that cherry for you, it's your new nickname." Finn grinned mischievously.

"You were listening in on our conversation and you knew when to come scare me!" I screeched.

"We haven't had this much fun in a while," Sean chuckled, closing the door to the roof.

"Here, take this bag and stay in between the two of us. We'll keep you safe."

"Somehow, I doubt that's your first priority," I mumbled, hefting the lightest bag that they'd left for me.

"Did you get the other bags from our apartment?" Sean asked Finn as we made it down the two flights of stairs.

"Yeah, I took your bag down there. Caleb's got everyone gathered outside waiting on us," Finn assured us.

The sunlight hit my face, and I had never been so glad that I wasn't a vampire in my entire life. While hanging outside wasn't top on my priority list, living in the pitch dark with infected things wandering around was something I really wanted to avoid.

"Everything okay?" Darren questioned as we carefully placed the bags in the back seat of the truck.

"Yep. Is there any way we could find a parts store on the way back? I might be able to work something out with your energy levels and get you electricity that doesn't have to be rationed."

"Let's wait until we get back to the church, then you can take a look at the setup. Some of their equipment is really old, and might not connect with whatever you pick up. Plus, we've got orders to get food supplies, and there's a store nearby that hasn't been hit yet. That has to be our priority today," Darren insisted.

"If these guys are as good as they say they are, this might just be the edge we need to survive," Tony declared as we made our way out the back of the complex, pulling the gate closed behind us.

Chapter 6

Cole

The two groups had both brought back a few survivors, but this also meant that it would drain our supplies much faster than before. Any life that was saved would be useful, but there would have to be some order to the chaos.

River got together with Sarah Beth, Lee's girlfriend, and they started dividing up the people.

I watched, amazed, as she jumped in without asking, making everyone feel at home while directing them to something that would benefit the general group.

"Lee, I think we need to have a meeting tonight with the main game-players about how this can work if you want us to stay around to help you."

"You'd stay and help us get things going?" Lee

asked, incredulous.

"It's an option. If we just take back the one's our group came for, we're bringing at least ten people to the mountain, if not more. While resources aren't really a problem there at the moment, you need more people to help clear things out. If we can get a set area that's free of infected, we might be able to start doing some trade again between farms and other places."

"We'll need to run it by the girls, and I think we need a clear plan on how to reach the goal of putting the lights back on and getting things back open in a semblance of normal," Darren agreed.

"A meeting after dinner would be good in the sanctuary so we can get everyone's thoughts." Lee seemed excited about the prospect.

"While I'm all for a democracy, I think we need to have a smaller planning group. River, Stacy, Andi, Sarah Beth, Darren, me, you, and Sean should be enough to put a plan together before we present it to everyone. Too many chiefs and nothing gets accomplished," I cautioned.

"I see what you mean. After we map out a plan, we should present it to the entire group and let them vote or make other suggestions as well. I'd also like Tony to be present to represent our veterans so they aren't left out."

"Works for me."

I wandered over to where Sean was working to put his computer system back together.

"Need any help?" I hated to be sitting around doing nothing.

"Actually, yes. I need to find a way to put this on the outside facing the sun. From the way we came in, I'm guessing that we don't really have access to the outside of the building. We can run the wires anywhere, but obviously, they need to see the sun."

"It might require a little work, but I think that can be arranged. Let me go ask Lee if he has a specific place for that to happen."

Turning away from Sean, I called out, "Hey, Lee? Where do you want to put the gamers so they're not disturbed, but have access to the outside for their solar panel?"

"They have a solar panel, and they're going to use for video games?" I couldn't believe what I was hearing.

"Uh, I think that might be the best way to keep them out of the way."

"Cole, don't be silly. You should have seen the setup they have, not only with power, but with plants as well. Once Sean gets a system setup here, they plan to go back over there to live," Andi informed him.

I should have expected her to be listening in since she'd done it from birth, but she still caught me off-guard sometimes.

"The best place to make a command center would be over in the church building. There are rooms up on the second and third floors that have access to the windows, and it would be far enough away from where the kids are playing ball so they wouldn't hurt anything," Lee suggested. "I'm really starting to hate this being in charge thing," he muttered.

"Don't let River hear you saying that, or I have a suspicion that she'll take you up on it if you're offering," I chuckled.

The meeting of the group leaders went a lot more smoothly than I had anticipated.

Stacy wasn't going to go back to the mountain without Darren, and while he would have been a nice addition, the church could use him more than the mountain could.

River wanted to be part of the action and felt comfortable with Stacy, so that put another one up for staying.

Sean was staying in town with his family, which meant that Andi would stay since she had a crush on him, and I was going to stay and watch over her.

"We need a plan going forward from here." Lee had a small speaker stand that made him seem like the preacher in the small conference room.

"The rescue missions are going to do to things to our facilities, cause them to overflow with very desperate people, and spread our resources very thin."

"May I make a suggestion?" River's hand shot up at the same time she spoke.

"Yeah." Lee's eyes widened when she came to stand next to him at the podium.

"The military had the correct idea of securing a strong building to house people. The kids who've been here for over a month now are about to go crazy inside, and the parents and grandparents aren't far behind them. Now we've added a few extras, and I'm sure if we were to go to different neighborhoods, we'd find about ten people in each that have made it this far. That's not going to continue as people eat through their stockpiles and that of their dead neighbors'." River's hands moved as she spoke to emphasize her words.

"I think our focal point should be on finding an area that has few dead people and clear that out like you've done with most of the downtown. If we can include a park or play area, that would be a huge asset," Stacy chimed in, backing up River's thoughts.

"Our biggest problem with trying to clear out highly populated areas is that we don't have the weapons or the trained manpower for that kind of operation," Lee protested.

"Lee, you and I both know that putting guns in the hands of untrained people can cause just as many casualties as it would be helpful." Sarah Beth let out a sigh.

"Okay, I'm new here, but my friends and I have a few skills that can be helpful. Not only are we tech-savvy, but we were all taking some different engineering classes. Finn was a double major as an electrical engineer and IT, which he did just for fun. Caleb was an agricultural mechanics and sciences major. He was our plant guy. Rob was working on his second degree in environmental energy since he'd finished his environmental development degree two years ago."

"You'd like us to believe that the stoner-gamers all

had the motivation to get not one, but two different degrees?"

"Yep. What can I say? We were bored after the first one, but our parents were expecting us to attend school for four years or more. We didn't want to disappoint their expectations."

I exchanged glances with Darren and Lee. If these guys could do even half of what they were claiming, then we might have a chance to put the world back together again. Since when had I begun including Lee in my circle of approved people?

"Can you make solar power for our buildings so that we can quit using fuel and keep that for the vehicles?" River brought everyone back to the task at hand.

"I believe so. There are a few areas that have more energy efficient homes in the area, and we can do one of two things with them. First, clear them out and put people groups in them, and then we can look for the local provider who should have extra panels stored in a warehouse. Once the communication channels are available, it'll be easier to coordinate between the small communities that we setup."

"We're missing a part of the equation here. We need medical staff to make sure that we stay healthy. There isn't anything to tell us how this virus got started, and most of those that were trained are dead since they were called into the hospitals and clinics to help the infected before they were overrun," Sarah Beth pointed out.

"Those are going to be few and far between in the near future, but hopefully the military can start training some individuals. Our friend Angela is a nurse, but she could at least help diagnose minor ailments."

"Ed, the guy we brought with us today, had a bad cough. I couldn't leave him there, but what if he'd had the infection? We have no idea on how to treat it. What can we do in this instance so that we don't get all the others killed?"

"I asked him some questions because I was worried about that very thing. The cough medicine seemed to work, but we put him in a room by himself," Sarah Beth reassured us.

"Can we have someone that patrols the sleeping quarters at night just in case something like this were to happen? I don't want us to jump from the frying pan into the fire," I suggested helpfully.

"Certainly. It makes good sense anyway, in case someone was trying to sneak into the building or out of it. At the moment, we haven't come across any of the more violent elements that could be harmful to the community, but the more we grow, the more likely it'll happen. We don't want to be unaware of what's going on around us, either." Lee tried to take the meeting back, but at this point, even though he and River were standing at the podium, it had become a group discussion.

More ideas were thrown out and dismissed, or details worked out, but after two hours, I couldn't take anymore.

"Is there a point we can take this up again in about a week? I don't know about the rest of you, but I'm exhausted and would like a chance for some down time."

"Lee?" River moved the ball back into his court.

"Nope, I'm good. Let's go with this plan for the next few days, and if we have any large things we need to adjust, we can have a small meeting."

"Great. Sarah Beth, can we go check on Ed to make sure he's okay?" River had taken charge, and no one else in the room even realized that they had been prodded in the direction that she wanted them to go.

I followed them out, intending to keep an eye on them while they talked to Ed, but Darren stopped me.

"Go get some shut-eye. I'll take the first walking shift tonight. I'd rather sleep when Stacy does if that's okay with you?"

"Yeah, dude." I covered the yawn that was trying to escape. "I guess you have the right idea. Night."

The room I'd been in had two cots, but at the moment, I was the only occupant. If the planning group had anything to say, we would have to start rotating our sleeping areas into shifts to accommodate all the people they hoped to find alive.

I was a bit more of a cynic, and didn't find that dreaming about the future was enough to keep me awake as my head hit the pillow.

Chapter 7

One Month later…

River

My eyes opened as the sound of eerie music filled the room. It sounded like a pipe organ was playing quietly throughout the building in the middle of the night.

I sat up, swinging my legs over the side of the cot, and slid my feet into the no lace tennis shoes. There wasn't much light that filtered into inner classrooms, but it also meant there was less chance for a ZIT to attack.

The door opened without squeaking as I clutched the bat in my hand and followed the music.

Noise would attract the ZITs, and I couldn't

imagine anyone intentionally playing an organ in the dark as I felt my way to the stairs.

The closer I crept to the sanctuary, the louder the strains of a song about Christian unity and love echoed around me.

Had no one else heard the music? Was I finally going nuts and it was all in my head?

As the last note died out, a scuffling scrape came from the platform, and I gripped the bat tighter.

A hand reached to cover my mouth, and with a small gasp, I turned to find myself staring into the blue eyes of Cole.

Ugh! At least I knew I wasn't crazy, but I must have been radiating anger because he dropped his hand from my mouth before I could bite him.

"Sorry. It's Gerald. He thinks if he plays at night no one will know," Cole whispered inches away from my mouth.

"Unless he knows how to hook up a hundred-year-old organ to headphones, people are going to hear him." I inwardly groaned as my body started to realize there was a healthy man standing in front of me.

I turned to go stop Gerald from playing, but Cole placed a hand on my arm. "He only plays that one song."

"You mean, I've slept through that every night?" I asked, a little incredulous.

"Evidently. I'm sure you need your beauty sleep, Angel," Cole chuckled in the darkness.

I wanted to slap the smugness I knew was on his face, but it would only encourage him more.

Since the moment we'd met a few weeks ago, he'd been constantly telling me I was pretty or beautiful. Seriously, we were in the middle of the ZIT apocalypse, and this guy was acting like we were just going to start dating. Plus, the nickname he'd come up with for me was just a little obnoxious—Angel.

"Look, Cole, I don't know how many times your small amount of manhood can take being rejected, but it's going to keep happening. I'm not your Angel or anyone else's. If I even have a halo up there, it's being held up by horns, and my tale has quite a sting to it, so can you back off?" Exasperated, I didn't know how else to explain to him that it just wasn't going to happen.

He leaned against the open door. "I adore your horns because they're cute. Besides, you have a lot more good in you than you think. Not once have you complained about our situation, or the things the other girls worry about."

"Wait a second…so you're telling me that you like the fact that I'm not into lots of makeup or cry when I break a nail?" I simply couldn't fathom a man that wasn't focused on a girl with assets.

"Yep. Makeup isn't all it's cracked up to be. Don't get me wrong, if a woman wants to wear makeup, dye her hair and get her nails done, I'm all for it if that's what she wants. Wash all that off and you'll find out more about the real person underneath."

"Oh, so anyone that uses makeup to look better and not scare the human race should just forget it because we just need to look at their hearts? Did they even let you date when you were in the military? I can't imagine that you've had experience with many women with attitude." I tried to move through the doorway, but he blocked me with his body.

"Cole?"

"We can discuss my experience or preferences all day long, but until you let me in past those walls you've built, it doesn't matter who I've dated before. I've sampled all sorts of women who were willing, but they're not the kind of girls who could hold my attention for very long. Cheesy as it sounds, I've wanted to kiss your bare lips since the moment I saw you."

A shiver ran down my arms as he took the bat from my hands and ran a finger under my chin. I'd never been wanted for just being me. It was always some guy trying to get a quickie and move on to the next conquest.

He leaned closer and I didn't stop him, but jumped when his lips gently touched mine. Tenderness wasn't something I'd expected from him, but I found myself responding.

When he pulled back, it left me breathless.

"What is it?" I assumed he'd stopped because I had done something wrong.

"Nothing."

"Why'd you stop then?"

"Because I wanted to give you a chance to say no before I continued. I'm all about mutual consent."

Cole was one of the few honorable men I'd come across, and this was my chance to overlook his constant banter. No one had been able to make me feel scared and excited all at the same time. Forgetting all about Gerald and the reason for our meeting here in the first place, I pulled him into the room and to the pews.

"I consent," I whispered before I let down my guard and embraced the moment to let him in, just a little.

Morning after regrets were horrible, but I'd hoped that Cole would take the hint and keep our little session secret.

My face blushed as I realized exactly how there were really horns on my head. We'd done it in a church sanctuary. Bright side, we hadn't been struck by lightning, so maybe we weren't the first to do it there.

If I delayed leaving to go downstairs, then maybe he would already be gone by the time I showed up.

A knock on the door had me wishing a zombie would attack just so I didn't have to answer it and face whoever was on the other side.

Stacy's head appeared, and I sighed in relief.

"You okay?" she asked, closing the door to give us some privacy.

It was a reasonable question since I was laying on the bed fully dressed.

"Yeah," I mumbled. "It was a long, restless night. I'm just trying to psych myself up enough to be around people today."

"So Cole is really getting under your skin, huh?"

"What?" I sat up quickly and tried to figure out how

she knew about Cole.

"River, we've all seen the way you two react to each other. We're just placing bets on when you'll actually give in and do it." Stacy grinned as she took a seat on the end of the cot.

"He's really into you, and you can't hold out on his handsome face forever. Although, he does come up with some great pickup lines."

"What I'm wondering is, did any of those ever really work in the pre-ZIT world?" I pulled my legs up to make more room for Stacy.

She giggled. "Honestly, I think he's using them to get your attention. The big question is, are you going to do something about it, or just leave him walking around with a lost puppy face?"

"He has a lost puppy face?" I asked, perking up.

"Every time someone walked into the room this morning and it wasn't you, he'd frown and go back to eating. He's got a bad case of the wannas."

"The wannas?" I knew that I wasn't always up on the most popular sayings, but this one was completely new.

"Yep, the 'I wanna do you all night long.'"

"Oh my gosh. Really? Can everyone just grow up and leave us alone?"

"No way," Stacy exclaimed, grinning.

"Huh?" My head was starting to hurt from all the emotions I normally held inside.

"You already did it with him, didn't you?" She wagged a finger in my face.

"Yes, okay. This is the reason I so didn't want to get involved with someone. It's way too complicated. I don't want to deal with all this stuff." I groaned and pulled the pillow over to cover my face.

"So if I told you that Cole is already gone, and we girls are going to go kill some zombies, there's no way you'd be up for that, right?"

I raised my head. "You know what? That's exactly what I need today. I need to kill something and get that man right out of my head."

"That a girl. We're sneaking out and heading toward the edge of the city to see if we can find some gardens or farms that might have some worth."

Throwing the pillow behind me, I jumped up and picked up the bloodstained bat from the floor. "Let's go pop some ZITs."

"Yes, ma'am." Stacy saluted and followed behind me.

"I know there were several families and groups that were alive when I came down from Bethel two months ago. Unless they tried to go into town, they should still be on their farms, and the infected won't be wandering the woods."

"You can be our peace offering and work something out to exchange goods. Although, I don't know what we could offer those on the farms, even if they are willing to trade for food. Winter's going to come and we're not going to have the option of a stockpile ready to keep everyone warm and fed."

"Most of our farm families could use extra labor for free. I think it should be mostly the guys that we send to help them, because if we send any women, there's no telling if they'll be safe." Seeing the looks on our faces, Sarah Beth hurried to explain further. "No, the farmers wouldn't necessarily do anything, but they would be willing to trade them to someone bigger and stronger if they came along and wanted them. The fact that it would keep their own families safe would be the main reason for something like that to happen."

"That's completely barbaric," Stacy exclaimed, horrified.

"Well, just because we don't like it, doesn't mean it doesn't make sense. These mountain people are loyal to family, but outsiders can't be trusted, so they can be traded for something that's worth it to the group's greater good."

"So what you're saying is, don't piss these farmers off because they might kidnap us and sell us off to the highest bidder?" I couldn't keep the fear off my face. It was way more than I'd planned on for a day outing.

Sarah Beth thought there were a few farms that might still have people there, but they were empty, with no signs of ZITs.

In a couple of places, we were excited to find animals grazing out in the pastures, still alive.

"What should we do with these, guys? We can't just leave them out here to fend for themselves. I don't believe their owners have been gone too long, but they do have fresh water in the pond." Stacy patted the friendly horse's mane.

"My Uncle John's house is only a few miles over. If he's still there, he can send one of the boys up the mountain for help." Sarah Beth had full confidence that her uncle would be willing to help.

"How can you be so sure that they'll help us out? Why would they even want to? It's safer up there where there aren't any ZITs trying to kill them." I still wasn't used to people trying to help others without something exchanging hands.

"These are farms that need people to take care of them. There are so many extra people up there, which is why we send some down here to live, and if the farm land is open, they'll jump on it. Plus, there are animals that need taken care of, and nothing bothers a farmer worse than animals that will starve if someone doesn't help them." Sarah Beth grinned just thinking about the opportunities her community had available now. "Besides, if someone doesn't warn them, and by some crazy chance a zombie does make it up there, they need to know how to kill it. I don't want them to be defenseless."

"That makes sense," I agreed. "I'll reserve judgement until we see if they come down and work with these animals. How many farms have we cleared out that had animals that were still alive, or crops that needed to be harvested soon?"

"I have a list put together on a spreadsheet of all the assets we've found. I've been using the truck to keep the laptop charged, and when we come back, I'm updating it.

All I'll have to do is upload it to Sean, and we can find people who know how to run the machinery, or if they can learn it easily. Some of the older people may have more experience, but then again, they're all city people," Andi informed us. Our jaws dropped.

"Don't look so shocked. Just because there isn't internet access, doesn't mean that I can't use my tech skills for good. I've listened over the years on Jackson Mountain, and may have picked up a few things about crops and animals. Doesn't mean that I want to milk a cow, but I know someone who does." She grinned and pointed to a map on her computer. "Is this where your uncle lives?"

Sarah Beth glanced at it. "Yep. What's this over here?"

I followed her finger to a star on the map about thirty miles from where we were at, if I was reading it correctly.

"That's Jackson Mountain. So if your people don't come down, or we can't fill all those farms because we don't have enough people, I have a solution." Andi gave River a mischievous grin.

"There are way too many people on the mountain, and while it was a good idea to rally around in a safe place, I guarantee that Cole will be more than willing to talk some of the family into spreading out."

"Cole." I rolled my eyes. "You know he's never going to let me out of his sight again. I'm pretty sure he thinks that because we did that together last night, that I need to be near him at all times."

"Honestly, I know the guys can seem pretty intense, but they just don't know how to deal with us. It's so ingrained in them to protect people. I mean, that's what they've done day and night for years, but then suddenly, they're supposed to turn that off like a switch. They can't do it with civilians, so imagine how much harder that is when it's someone they love," Stacy argued, wanting us to see things from their point of view.

"He can't love me yet. I'll admit that he has strong feelings. I guess that in the long run, overprotective is better than someone who doesn't really care. He's just going to have to tone it down. I haven't had anyone care for me in a long time. I have no idea how to react when someone gets close to me," I confessed, bewildered at the whole idea of love.

"Ha! Cole isn't one of those that'll let go. He's decided that you're the one he wants, and I don't think he's going to let that spark die out," Sarah Beth giggled.

"The sparks were nice." I could feel my face turning

red.

"Don't worry, he can be very patient. Remember that I've grown up with him and my dad trying to protect me. Cole is the better at dealing with emotions than my dad. It could be because he's not my dad, but honestly, he's always been able to figure out what I need and calmed dad down from doing something crazy," Andi explained.

"Talk to him. Tell him what you're thinking, because contrary to common opinion, men can't actually read our minds. You're going to have to get vulnerable and let him in," Stacy advised wisely.

"That's easier said than done. Can't I just keep using him as my hot sex toy? I'd much rather get naked than talk about my feelings." I groaned at the thought of having this type of conversation with him.

My attention drifted as I saw smoke coming through the trees.

"Stop the truck."

Sarah Beth slowly came to a stop. "What do you see?"

"Smoke. It's through there. Can we find a road and see if we can see what's causing it?" I pointed slightly behind us to an area that had been hidden from the road by trees.

"Um, there's a road about a half a mile behind us that should lead to a house over that way," Andi advised, consulting the map.

"Even though there aren't a lot of cars around, I'm going to go over the hill and find a place to turn around that's wider. These two-lane roads aren't big enough to do a U-turn on, but there should be a driveway somewhere." Sarah Beth started forward while looking for a way back to follow the smoke.

She had gotten more practice driving since the zompoc started than she normally did in an entire year of monthly visits.

"Do whatever makes you feel comfortable. It's not like there are any police officers out here to give us a ticket if we don't follow the driver's handbook." I wasn't one to cast judgment, since I didn't even have a license to drive.

"I can see the smoke too." Stacy pointed to the skyline that was barely visible through the trees.

We drove slowly down the dirt road until we came to a clearing that allowed us to see where the smoke was coming from—a cabin farther up the hill. The chimney was smoking away, signaling that there were people alive.

"Not many people would have a fire going in the middle of summer because it's too hot. Most cabins don't have air conditioners, and it wouldn't work way out here anyway because the electric should be out this far out," Sarah Beth cautioned as we continued driving closer.

"Be on the lookout for anyone in the woods, or anything that seems a little funky."

Stacy held up the rifle we'd brought with us and looked through the scope.

"I don't see anything out of the ordinary. There's a truck parked up there, but it's empty."

"Let's park in the trees and walk the last little bit up to the cabin, just to be on the safe side," I suggested, feeling more comfortable with my bat rather than a gun.

"Good plan," Andi seconded from beside me.

Sarah Beth pulled over and turned the truck off. "Don't shut the doors all the way. We don't want to alert whoever's inside that we're out here," she cautioned us as we got out.

Chapter 8

It felt so good to stretch from being in the truck for the past few hours. I was moving around, walking the blood back into circulation, when we heard the door to the cabin creak open.

"Who's out there?" a younger voice called out. "We need help. If you're here to rob us then you're out of luck. We don't have any food. Be careful of the traps we set."

"He warned us. That's gotta count for something, right?" I looked at the others to see what their thoughts were on the situation.

"If it's a trick, we won't know until we get closer." Stacy tilted her head to the side, waiting for the rest of us to decide.

"Let's do it." Sarah Beth motioned us forward.

There was no point in trying to be quiet, so we

moved over to the dirt road and walked right up to the cabin.

"I see you've got guns, but don't shoot us, please." The voice opened the door and stepped out.

He was a younger teen, about fourteen, who looked starved.

"Is there anyone else inside with you?" Stacy asked gently, not wanting to startle him.

"Yeah, it's just me and Billy. He got hurt, and I think his leg is broken. Is one of you a nurse?" he asked, sounding hopeful.

"No, but let's take a look. Have you eaten recently?" I couldn't help seeing his arm shake as he lowered the gun.

"No. I didn't want to leave Billy for very long in case he turned into one of the dead. I didn't have anything left to put in the traps." He walked back inside, leaving the door open for us to follow him inside.

"Andi, can you run out to the truck and get the first aid bag and the food pack?" I didn't know what else we'd need, but those two things should get us started.

"Yeah, sure." She turned and took off to get what we needed.

"What's your name, honey?" Sarah Beth asked the

young boy.

"Carson. We've been in this cabin about three weeks now. The others didn't make it, and I didn't know how to get back to where we started."

His head turned as Andi came racing back into the room.

"Try this." She held out a bottle of water. "Sip it slowly, and then try this orange. We found it a few farms over this morning."

She uncapped the bottle because his hands were shaking so bad, and held it to his mouth.

"How's Billy doing?" Carson asked after several bites of the orange.

"He has a broken leg, but it's infected. We don't have any way to fix him here. The church has some medicine, but we don't have a doctor who could make any decisions about this." Sarah Beth gave a worried glance down at Billy's leg.

"Should we try and take him back to the church?" I asked, hoping that we weren't inviting death into our home.

"I know where there's a doctor or a nurse. I don't know if she'd come here, but I can use the walkie and see if they'll answer," Andi offered.

"Cole's not going to like it, though," I argued.

"Yeah, well, that's not something that you've cared about until now. I'll go out there and see if I can get them to come here." She went out the front door so Carson couldn't hear her conversation.

"Why did you have a fire going? That's how we knew someone was here," I questioned gently.

"It's been so cold at night, and I was afraid to let it go out because we ran out of matches. If we did catch something, there would be no way to cook it, and I really had nothing else to do anyway." He gave a shrug. "There's a pump outside with a well, I think, but I didn't want to drink water that was contaminated, so I've been boiling it. I've been so hungry that I couldn't even go out there to do that for the past few days."

"It's okay," I assured him. "We'll make sure that you get some real food in your stomach once that gives you a sugar boost. We don't want to overwhelm your system and make you sick."

Andi came back in the room, looking nervous. "They're coming."

"The way you said that sounded really ominous. Are they going to kidnap us after they help?" I asked.

"No." Stacy shook her head at Andi's dramatics.

"I wasn't there long, but what Andi's really worried

about is that her dad's going to come and chew her out for leaving in the middle of the night. He would never have agreed to his daughter going out to try and find Sean and Sam," Stacy explained.

"He's had more than a month to get un-mad. He needs to learn to chill. I called him when I needed help," Andi grumbled.

"The doctor is coming, though, right?" Sarah Beth asked.

"Yeah, and they're bringing antibiotics and other medical stuff. Doug is going to escort them, along with my dad."

"Angela's not a doctor, though. She took care of about everything that most doctors did. At least she'll know more about what we're looking at than any of us do," Stacy reckoned.

"If we can get Billy fixed up, can you guys help us get back to my mom? She's part of a co-op over in the next county," Carson asked, looking up from eating more of the fruit that we'd found.

"That'll all depend on if she's still staying where you left her, sweetie. You don't know that she'll be alive or in the same spot that you were since it's been over three weeks." I didn't sugarcoat it, because after what he'd seen the last few weeks, that was the last thing he needed.

"No, you don't understand. We have a community. A town with lots of people who are alive. We made it out of the city when the zombies first got started and have been on my aunt's farm since the beginning. Her boyfriend, Linc, gathered the town, and we have several farms working over there," Carson informed us.

"A community? How many people are alive? That's a small miracle these days."

I wanted him to keep talking without realizing that we were pumping him for information.

"About half the town survived, but they had to get rid of Jim Danvers because he let Linc's mom die. Since then, we've cleared out the farms, and they were just teaching us how to put in solar panels. We were supposed to go to the other towns and install them, but the other guys thought we needed alcohol for that since there would be other teens to party with." Carson paused. "Can I have another bottle of water? Please?" he added as an afterthought.

"He's got manners. Sure, kid. Just remember, take it slowly."

I knew telling that to a teenage boy who hadn't eaten in a while was like telling the sun it couldn't shine again. It was going to happen, but at least I'd warned him.

"Did you find the alcohol you were looking for?" Andi asked curiously.

"Yeah, it's out in the truck. They had a shack out in the woods with a hidden stash that someone would bring them. We loaded it up, but heard something in the trees. They didn't listen when I told them it was probably the infected, and that we should get out of there." Carson stopped, looking like he might cry.

"It's okay. Honey, you did the best you could to warn them. They just didn't listen." Stacy placed a hand on his shoulder in comfort.

"No, it's my fault. I told them I was fifteen, but I'm only thirteen. Tina had the hots for me, and we'd been making out on the way over with the others. When we got to the building, she wanted us to go out back and drink and stuff..." He trailed off, blushing.

"Oh, she wanted to do it, but you weren't ready yet?

"Uh-huh. It just didn't feel right. The others had brought another girl, and they were all telling me to do it. I just couldn't. So she took Ben behind the shack, and we could hear them while we finished loading things up. Then the infected came out of the trees." He blushed again. "She was really loud and drawing them to us. Then she started really screaming, and they were both being attacked. I knew there wasn't anything we could do for them, so the rest of us got in the truck. We killed a few of them as we got the truck going, but she stopped screaming."

"Carson, it's really okay to cry. No one here is going to think less of you." Andi walked over and sat right in front of him.

"Never mind, you need just need a hug." She surprised all of us by grabbing him and holding him for a minute. "There, I feel better now."

He sniffled. "Uh…yeah, me too."

"It's not your fault she was a witch with a capitol B, dude," Sarah Beth chimed in, as Andi sat back on the floor, patting his leg.

She kept surprising me with her compassion and common sense. I just hoped that her dad realized what a unique daughter he had.

"We made it here, but Wendy and Cox went out to check the traps about two weeks ago with me and Billy. We heard screams, but all we could do was shoot them because the infected had already killed them. When a bush rustled, Billy panicked and fell, breaking his leg. It was just a rabbit, but I helped get him back to the house and we bandaged him up.

"I went back out and dug two graves, dragging them back here. Since then, I found a few things in the traps, and we ate all the cans that were here those first few days. Billy started getting worse, and I didn't want to get attacked, so we didn't venture far."

"You did amazing. Most kids your age wouldn't have been able to keep anyone alive, much less someone else that was hurt," I consoled, trying to be reassuring.

"We were just sneaking out for a few hours. It wasn't supposed to go like this. There were several huge groups of dead that we had to go around, and I knew that if I got out there and tried to drive back, we'd get caught, and I wouldn't be able to get away."

"I'm sure that your mom is worried, and they've been looking for you ever since you left."

"I kept hoping that they'd come, but after the first two weeks and they didn't, I knew we were on our own. I was just waiting for Billy to die. I was going to bury him, and then see if I could find a way back. It would've been easier to find food in a house somewhere, and maybe a map."

"Do you remember the name of the town near the farm where you live?" Andi asked.

"Something like Teague, or League. I don't know.

We just always said we were going to go to town. They never really talked about a name for it since we all knew what they meant," Carson explained.

"You keep saying 'they.' Who is they?" I wondered just how many this really was since he'd said half the town was still alive.

"Well, there's my mom and three siblings. My aunt, two cousins, Linc and his three guys, because one of them was killed by Jim Danvers. I think they were ex-military, because they trained us how to use guns and do patrols when we're not working on the farm. Aunt Jessica has cows and grows lots of stuff, so even though the infected are out there somewhere, we have to keep things growing."

"Oh, wow. That's a lot of people on one farm," Stacy commented, having no idea what it took to keep one running.

Sarah Beth stood up. "Did you give them directions on how to get here?"

"Yeah, why?"

"Because someone just pulled up, and these guys don't look like what you've described as your family." She pointed out the dirty window. Lifting her gun, she was getting ready for whatever was about to walk through the door.

"They're not from Jackson Mountain. I know just about everybody, and should recognize at least one person."

Andi picked up the walkie. "Dad? How far away are you?"

"We're about ten minutes out. We ran into a herd of those ZITs." Dawson's voice came through the radio.

I pulled the gun from the waistband of my pants. "Stop right there!" I yelled, cracking the door just a little bit.

"We've got you covered, so introduce yourselves."

"Hey, now. We saw the smoke and thought we'd come over and help," one of the six guys approaching answered back, lowering his weapon.

"Stay back and shoot them if they make a move," I whispered to the girls as I stepped out onto the porch.

"What do you want?" I kept the gun trained on what appeared to be the leader.

"Just being neighborly." The leader made a motion with his hand, and the others started to spread out.

I aimed in the general direction of the one closest to the side of the cabin. "I said stop. That means, don't try to flank me."

Andi was talking softly to her dad on the radio,

telling him what was going on.

"Now, now, that's no way to treat a neighbor. Figured you might need some help," he scoffed.

"We never said we needed help. The smoke's been going for three weeks now, and you just showed up? That seems awful suspicious, wouldn't you say?" I questioned, hoping to stall them until the cavalry got there.

"That's my fault, ma'am," a different man answered, taking his cap off in a gentlemanly gesture.

"There are just so few people out here in this new world, that we wanted to make sure that you have the protection you need."

I pointed to the gun in my hand. "I can assure you that I can take care of myself just fine, and the only person that's going to need protection is the guy who's moving to my right. I really suggest that you don't move again. I aimed for you the first time, I won't be so nice the next time. In fact, I think you should move over and stand next to your buddies."

He looked to the leader, who shrugged, before he moved a few feet back toward their vehicle.

"What did you want in exchange for this protection that you thought I so desperately needed from you?"

"Oh, there's safety in numbers, ma'am, and we

have a group that's been together since the start. We collect those that can't take care of themselves in this crazy place with dead walking around."

"I haven't heard anything that would sell me on what you're offering. I'm going to have to pass today. You can go on back to wherever you've been camped out."

They made no move to get back in their trucks until I took another shot at the leader, narrowly missing his head.

"Whoops. Guess I'll have to practice some more. I was aiming for a little lower on your body." I was keeping a straight face, but could hear the snickers from inside.

"That's it, boys. Go get those girls. I'm tired of being nice," the leader ordered his men.

The door had barely shut when the windows shattered, as Sarah Beth, Andi, and Stacy each took a shot at the unsuspecting guys.

"Just wound them. Let's not kill them until we have to," I ordered, using the small window in the door to see what was going on outside.

The unwelcome visitors had pulled their wounded comrades behind the vehicle, out of range. They hadn't started returning fire, but that didn't mean they weren't trying to sneak around the cabin.

"Carson, is there a back door in this place?"

"No, just a small bathroom with a little window. I don't think anyone could fit through it."

"Here, take my bat and wait in there, just in case. We need another set of eyes so they don't surprise us."

He eagerly took it from me and hurried to the bathroom. It was amazing what a little food and water could do to restore someone's health. Although kids recovered much faster than adults, and this way, he would be out of harm's ways if bullets started flying back at us.

"Any sign of them?" Stacy scanned the yard for signs of movement.

"Nope."

"Maybe I should let my dad know we hit a few of them." Andi picked up the walkie.

"Don't," I cautioned. "I think that's how they found us."

"Crap. And then I gave them directions on how to get here."

"I'm sure they thought a woman with a hurt man wouldn't be well armed, and they could have taken you before reinforcements got here."

"Not quite what they were expecting, huh?" Sarah Beth grinned at the thought.

"Oh, I've got something." Stacy directed our

attention. "To the left. If it's not your family, Andi, then the infected have discovered us, and we're about to be invaded."

A few shots rang out, then there was complete silence.

"Andi, you in there, sweetie?" a male voice called out.

"Dad! Did you find the six guys that were out there?" she responded, but we waited to see what he was going to say before we just rushed out there.

"No. There are two dead out here from bullet wounds. Looks like they snuck back to their vehicle and took off. Can we come in now?"

Andi pulled open the door and jumped into his arms. "I'm sorry. Please don't be mad at me."

"Aw, sweetie. I was, but I knew that Cole was with you, and if you had to go and rescue people, he's one of the few I would trust you with. Now these yahoos that showed up a few minutes ago are from a town farther south. I recognized Zeke, who's dead now, from a group we've run across as we've been searching for survivors."

"Oh, thank God. I don't think they had very good intentions." Stacy gave a relieved sigh.

"We've been wondering if they were listening in on

our frequencies. Most of what we do is now in code, but there was no way to find out where you were without exact directions," Andi's dad explained.

"Where's the patient?" Angela finally squeezed past the two blocking the doorway.

"Billy's over here. He's been out of it since we got here, but I figured that was from the infection." I walked with her to the bed, but went past to let Carson out of the bathroom.

"Hey, kid. It's okay to come out." I pushed in the door, only to find Carson shaking his head, a finger to his lips.

"One of those guys is creeping back to the front," he whispered.

"Andi's dad?" I called loudly.

He looked my way, only to see me frantically pointing to the side. He immediately understood and clicked the walkie twice.

We all stood there holding our breath, listening to the scuffle going on outside.

"Dawson, we got something you'll wanna see out here," someone called from outside.

We all trailed out with our guns to find one of the guys that had been trying to get inside tied up on the ground.

"Mick was coming around the house. Where did the rest of your group go?" Doug, Stacy's brother, questioned the captive.

"Noneya," Mick answered.

"Don't think that's exactly the answer we were going for. Try again." Doug pulled up on the rope holding his hands until they were in an awkward position.

"What's noneya mean?" Carson whispered to me.

"None of your business."

"Oh. I'll have to remember that and use it on my little sisters."

"Now, I'm gonna keep pulling up on this until I get an answer," Doug warned.

"No," Mick whimpered. "I'm just following orders."

"Whose orders?" Doug pressed.

"Vinnie's orders. He thought that we could take the girl by surprise. He's been trying to find a way to infiltrate your group or trade something that you wanted so that he could get the best of you."

"What else does he have planned?" Dawson interjected.

"He wants to get the food you have stored and a few

of the women so the guys will quit fighting." Mick winced as Dawson pulled a little harder than Doug had on the ropes.

"How many are in your camp?"

"I can't tell you that. Vinnie will have me killed."

"You have two choices: answer my questions and live for a while, or Vinnie can kill you as soon as you get back."

"That doesn't sound like a choice." Mick looked between the two guys, trying to decide which one was the one in charge.

Pushing through the testosterone, I figured I'd settle this for them. "Mick, is it?"

"Yeah," he gulped nervously.

"I'll make this even simpler for you. If you don't spill everything you know about Vinnie and his operation, then I use this bat on that sensitive area between your legs. I've heard it's not only painful, but that most men value it pretty highly." I swung the bat down into my hand, right in front of his face.

Since his hands were tied, he couldn't protect himself, except to move his knees closer together.

"Talk." I started to lean down and he gushed, trying to get words out before I brought the bat out to play.

"The camp is about ten minutes away from here. We change areas every week so that we can search for supplies. It's getting harder to find stores that aren't overrun with dead that we can get into for the food that's edible on the shelves. Vinnie thought we should start raiding farms and killing the animals."

"What would he do, because we showed up and they killed some of your guys?" Doug poked at Mick again.

"He's gonna be mad. He'll do pretty much anything, but he'll figure that your camp's easier to take over and head that way, hoping to ambush you on the way back."

"Tie him to the tree over there and watch him." Dawson ordered, walking back toward the cabin.

"Angie, how's the kid doin'?"

"I think he might survive with the antibiotics, but we need to get his leg off to be sure. I can give him a small dose to knock him out, but it needs to be a clean cut right above the knee." Angie pulled the blanket aside to show them the problem.

"You know what needs to be done." Dawson looked grim as he turned to Doug. "Let's carry him out to the truck bed. Go ahead and give him the medicine." Doug helped grab a few of the blankets off the floor and went outside.

I followed, curious what these two had planned.

"How are we going to keep Vinnie and his group from attacking us on the way to your camp?" I asked as I went to the truck the boys had arrived in to get a bottle of alcohol.

"We won't go the same way that we came. Now that we know where this is, we can take a back road and come around behind them. It's time we settled this. These guys have been following us around for weeks, and send ZITs toward us while they clear out whatever supplies we're about to take." Doug pulled an axe out of the back seat of their truck and held it out for me to pour the alcohol over.

"I wish we had something that hadn't been used to kill those infected things. It might not be completely clean, even with alcohol."

"Once we have it washed down, I'll go in there and put in the fire for a few minutes. Then we'll coat it again before we do it. Hopefully that'll be enough." Doug went back inside.

I'd seen and done a lot of stuff over the past few months, but this was by far the worse. I stayed out of the way as they moved poor Billy to the truck with his leg hanging off. It was when they started to untie Mick that I knew things were about to get messy.

This was more than I could do, so I went inside to stay with Carson while they took care of his friend.

"Are they going to take me back to my mom after they get Billy fixed up?" He got a little white as he thought about what they were doing.

"I don't think they're going to be able to take Billy back to your community today. This gang of Vinnie's would just follow, and then they might hurt your town. Dawson and Doug's group is going take them out while the rest of us get you and Billy back to their camp," I explained, not sure which group I'd be in—the one attacking or the escort.

"Will I ever be able to go back to my mom and siblings?" Carson looked to be on the verge of tears.

"Most of that will depend on what happens in the next few hours, but I want to get back to the church and Cole, so I'm going to bet that when us girls go back in that direction, we can make a slight detour." I was actually looking forward to seeing that pain in my butt guy.

Hearing only voices now and no screams, I looked out and could see that they were almost finished.

Doug came back toward the cabin and I opened the door.

"Should I put out the fire?" I didn't want to burn the place down. It wasn't like we had fire departments that could come and put it out if things spread.

"Dawson says leave it. It's pretty contained, and we don't want to signal that we're leaving. It might give us a few extra minutes of surprise on these guys." Doug took in the mostly empty room. "You're driving the truck Carson brought," he informed me.

"In all fairness, I don't have a license, but that hasn't stopped me yet." I grinned over at Carson, who suddenly laughed.

"Does that mean you're a good driver, or that you failed the test and can drive since there isn't parallel parking anymore?"

"This kid is smarter than I thought. I never tried, but now that there aren't any rules about driving down the middle of the road, I haven't had any problems." I shook my head, realizing why the others had thought he was older. It was because he was more mature than most high schoolers were.

We were the last ones to get in the trucks, and they had Mick with his hands tied in front of him, sitting next to Billy in the back to make sure he didn't get jostled around. He looked sick as he sat back there, paying attention to everything but Billy.

"Is it really a good idea to bring the prisoner with us?" I asked Doug as I walked over to the truck.

"We don't have much choice, and we can't leave him here. Plus, he'll make a good trade when we catch up to Vinnie's group."

"Okay. I'm not in charge, but anyone that tries to kill me unprovoked doesn't really get second chances in my book." I shrugged and got in the truck.

"Hey, kid, you'll have to hold my gun while I drive, and be on the lookout for anything out of place. Can you handle that?"

He nodded and slammed the door behind him. "Let's get this over with."

"Do they have someone watching the back way?" I asked, hoping we weren't going to get our heads shot at.

"Yeah, but they know we're coming and are on the lookout for us."

"How could they know that? We didn't radio them because of the other group listening in?" I turned to her, incredulous.

"Morse code, and a special set of instructions of code. These military, or ex-military guys, have a system that seems to work." Angie smiled.

Chapter 9

We had driven for about twenty minutes away from where Vinnie was expecting us, in the direction of the church, when we took a right and found a highway that was mostly empty.

This was where my new driving skills came in handy, because I had to avoid the infected, as well as the parked cars that had been abandoned with the doors open. It wouldn't have been as difficult, but with the doors open on most of the vehicles, there wasn't much space to squeeze through.

At the next major turn off, the group split up into two groups. Angie and Billy were moved over to our truck, while the other two trucks were ready to engage in a fight.

"Do you know where we're going?" I asked Angie, since I'd never been to Jackson Mountain.

"Yeah. I've been out with them a lot over the past two months. Most of them are pretty smart, but they wanted me to get the medical supplies that we could find and teach the others what to look for." Angie got a dreamy look on her face. "It didn't hurt that Doug was along, since I kind of have a crush on him. If things work out, then Stacy will actually be Dillon's aunt at some point. It's been a while since I had a man interested in me who cared about what happed to my kid as well."

"Angie, that's so exciting for you. Cole keeps trying to catch my attention by saying the most random things, or saying something that's going to make me mad because it's so macho. I ignored him for the longest time, and finally gave in the other night. Then I left him there with no clue that I was going to be gone for a few days. That'll show him."

"I've noticed that there are a lot more people hooking up with people that they never would have given a second glance to in the previous world." Angie sat with Billy's head in her lap, holding a pistol, ready in case we needed it.

"I think we've all realized that we could die at any moment and have to make the most of whatever opportunities we came across, be it love, infatuation, or just scratching an itch," I commented, keeping my eyes peeled for anything unusual since we were the only ones on the road now.

"The group on Jackson Mountain has been really inviting, but they did need some new blood to help pair off all those cousins. We don't want to become like that southern state, having kissing cousins marrying each other," Angie chuckled. "I'm only a nurse, but I know that inter-marriage between family members isn't the way to start over in this new world. Oh, there, take that road and go slowly until you reach the county road sign and take a left. We're going to come into the mountain roads from the back side," Angie directed from the backseat.

We pulled up to a dirt road with a gate and cattle guard. It wasn't until I started to get out of the truck that I realized that we were being watched.

"Hands in the air!" a voice called out, but I couldn't see anyone.

"Mason, it's us!" Angie shouted through the window.

The man peeled himself from the ground, behind what looked like a small fort that blended in enough that you wouldn't have seen him until you were already dead.

"Ah, you're River, the one that Dillion's been

talking about so much," Mason commented as he opened the gate for me to drive through.

Slamming the door, I pulled forward, muttering, "Why does everyone say it like that? Oh, you must be River. Do I have a wanted poster out that no one told me about?"

"No, sweetie. You're just a very visible individual. Even in the apocalypse, you've managed to keep your hair colored shades of green and blue. Plus, you win the hearts of everyone that comes in contact with you," Angie praised.

"But I'm not some kind of saint. I mean, I take people out with a bat. I have a weapon of choice. That's not someone that should be hailed a hero," I protested, uncomfortable with her words.

"Might as well get used to it, because when Dillion sees you, he's going to go crazy, and he could even give Cole a run for his money."

"How does everyone know that Cole has a thing for me? I swear, I'm going to run away so no one can find me. I'll become a hermit," I growled in frustration.

Carson raised his hand. "Can you take me home before you go all wild mountain animal?"

"Gracious. I give up." I shook a fist in the air to

whoever was up there listening.

Mason's son, Brad, had hopped in the back of the truck, and another camouflaged figure had taken his place at the gate.

He knocked on the window when we came to a fork in the road and pointed to the left, leading up the mountain.

"We have a cabin for those who are sick or injured in case they turn. We can't take any chances on an accident happening to those who are alive. Billy will be in good hands while you two walk up to the main house and see Dillion," Angie informed us.

"Have you heard anything from the other group yet?" I asked Brad, feeling like he was just an extension of Cole and Dawson.

"Nope. We've been keeping an eye out and nothing has happened at the two farthest checkpoints yet. Don't worry, they're trained to deal with guys much worse than these local yahoos," Brad assured me.

"Thanks. Carson, let's go get some food in you. I could use a chance to relax for just a little while. If we can, us girls will take you back tomorrow." I slung an arm over his shoulder, holding my bat in the other hand.

"You won't need that around here. We've got things covered." Brad motioned to the bat.

"Okay, Cole clone number two. While I appreciate that thought, I haven't gone anywhere without my bat in almost three months, and I don't plan to start now. Thanks, though." I left him standing there with his mouth gaping open, while Carson snickered.

A brown-haired woman in camo walked up, smiling. "You've done something I've never seen before. Brad's speechless. I'm Emma, Brad's wife, and it's about time someone shut these macho guys up. You must be River."

Carson burst out laughing. "Looks like you're gonna have to own it. Everyone knows you."

I didn't have a chance to respond before a solid body jumped at me. I almost swung my bat down, but managed to stop before I hit Dillion.

"Hey, buddy. How's it going?" I couldn't help but give him a hug.

"Mom's been here, but Stacy left and I miss her. There's kids to play with here, and I get to be outside." Dillion grabbed my hand, pulling me toward the house. "Come on, I've gotta show you where we get to play."

Stacy showing up would just make his world perfect, if they made it past Vinnie's men. I'd let her surprise him.

I'd spent so much time around Andi and Cole that the people living on the mountain seemed real, and I knew who everyone was from their descriptions.

After meeting all the kids and getting shown off, I went inside for some food, and to make sure Carson was being taken care of.

Nana shoved a plate of food and a fork in my hand.

"Mmm, this food is amazing," I mumbled, trying to talk with my mouth full.

Since I hadn't had a home in years, and there wasn't a chance to cook anything but cafeteria food after the zompoc, it was the best food I'd ever tasted.

"I never like anything I cook, but the kids seem to like it," Nana informed me.

"This shouldn't be wasted on children. I think you could be the top rated chef in a five-star restaurant. Although, you might be the only person that can do this anymore." I shoved another mouthwatering bite in, almost groaning out loud.

"Huh? Oh, I call all my children kids, even though

they have children and grandchildren of their own. No matter how old you get, you're still my kid." Nana pointed at the older people in the room.

"I didn't mean to offend you." I began to worry that I'd done something terrible. "It's just really good." I bit my lip, hoping nothing else would come out that could be misconstrued in a different manner.

"Don't sweat it, dear. Our family can be a little overwhelming. Although, I think you might be just the thing we need to shake things up a little bit." Nana patted me on the arm. "Have some dessert while we wait for the others to get back. I'd tell you to go get some rest, but you'd just lie there anxious until we knew everything was okay."

I didn't trust myself to answer, so I simply nodded.

This family was more intuitive than anything I'd ever seen, and when Andi had said they were always in your business, I had no idea what she'd meant, but it was quickly becoming clear.

The church ladies had made some wonderful desserts and food, considering they didn't have fresh dairy to work with, but nothing even came close to the heaven I was tasting with this cake.

"Why don't you take that outside on the porch and

sit with Emma while she feeds Pierce?" Nana suggested.

"Um, thank you." I walked out and found the porch miraculously deserted of extra people.

"Are there always so many people around?" I sat down in the chair to finish consuming the delicious cake.

"Hmm, I wish I could say that it's only because of the zombie apocalypse, but that's not true. Jackson Mountain has always had lots of people living here, or in and out all the time. They would move away, and yet they all come back at some point. It's like a beacon that beckons them home, especially when there's an emergency." Emma adjusted the blanket over her and the baby.

"I've always kept my amount of people interaction low until this thing happened, and now it seems like there are people around all the time. It's hard to get a moment alone," I admitted, as I sat the empty plate on the table in between the chairs next to my bat.

"This family is worse than the average one, because my mom would call every once in a while, but they're all nosey." She smiled, and a ball came flying past the edge of the house, followed by a kid retrieving it.

"The pros are that they love you enough to care and make sure that you're really okay. I don't know that Pierce and I would have survived if we hadn't been here. All it would take is for him to cry at the wrong moment and the infected would have been all over us."

"Yeah, I can see how that would be a good thing. Do they at least let you out of the house for guard duty? I feel like the men around here would be overprotective."

Emma let out a laugh. "If you could only hear some of the conversations that happen around this place, but the guys generally come around to our way of thinking. Brad wasn't here when it started, or we might've had a few more fights than we did since I was already in the rotation."

I got up and started pacing. "I can't stand just waiting around if there's something that can be done. I know those guys mean business, and we're just hanging out like it's just any other day."

A woman, a little older than me and Emma, came out and stood on the porch.

"You must be Haley, Andi's stepmom. She was really worried about her dad's reaction over leaving." I sat back down because it was harder to walk between the two ladies without bumping into them.

She pulled a vape device out of her pocket and took a puff, aiming it away from Emma and the baby.

"Andi may say she's scared or worried, but when it comes to standing up for herself, nothing can stop her from saying what she thinks. I knew that the people here would get on her nerves eventually. Up until the other group came back from Nashville, she didn't have an excuse to leave." She exhaled in a cloud of fumes, head bent over the railing, looking at the ground.

"She's not stupid, and knew that she couldn't take on those things out there without help. Cole is just the person to let her do what she wants. He's always given her anything she even thinks she might want. She was born while they were at boot camp, when Dawson's first wife was still around. All the guys doted on her because she was the first baby in the family since they'd been born, probably."

Haley's head came up suddenly. "Something's going on at the gate."

She took off running, and I wasn't far behind her as gunshots echoed through the trees.

Emma had jumped up and ran inside at the first sign of trouble. I was pleasantly surprised to see her catch up to us, holding an automatic weapon.

That was my idea of protecting the family, trading a baby in for a gun.

Chapter 10

Andi

We'd let the other group drive out of sight before we started circling back, hoping to catch Vinnie's group off-guard.

An exited tension filled the cab of the truck I was in, and for once I could appreciate the survival skills my dad insisted that we learn when we went to camp at Nana and Pop's house.

The radio crackled, and Vinnie's voice came over the radio. "Mick, do you read?"

Doug, who was riding in the back with Mick, held the radio up and gave him a warning. "You answer him and tell him where to pick you up. If you do that, then when he comes, we won't shoot you." Doug pressed the button as everyone held their breath.

"Yeah, I read you. I had to get far enough away that the other group wouldn't hear me." Mick shook nervously, watching the guns pointed at him.

"It's been a while. Can you make it to the crossroads? We're in the lookout building." Vinnie wasn't stupid, and didn't give out which road or building.

"'Bout another fifteen minutes and I'll be there. Once those guys showed up, there wasn't any way to move because they posted a lookout, but they finally left." Mick tried to keep talking, but Doug released the button.

"Idiot! You were supposed to let us know when they left. They didn't come this way so they must be on to us. Get your ass here, and if you aren't here in ten minutes, we'll leave you behind." Vinnie's anger could be felt through the radio.

"Yes, sir. I'm hurrying as fast as I can," Mick huffed into the radio.

Doug waited, but nothing else came through the speaker.

"He won't respond. He's probably trying to think of how to kill me now. Will we be there in ten minutes?"

"I don't know," Doug responded, getting in Mick's face. "Which crossroads is he talking about? What lookout building?"

"It's the next one, and there's a path through the woods from the gas station so that you won't be seen approaching until it's too 1-late," Mick stuttered, frightened of Doug.

"If you're leading us into a trap, it won't be Vinnie that kills you. It'll be me or my ghost, because I'll haunt you forever," Doug threatened.

Mick's head nodded so fast, spit flew everywhere. He was trying to keep everyone happy.

Doug waved once to the truck following us to pull over.

When we were parked and gathered around, Dad split us into three groups, sending mine and Doug's to get ready farther in the woods so Vinnie's group couldn't see us.

He was going to escort Mick up to the door of the lookout building.

"Be careful, Dad." I gave him a tight smile before I blended in with the trees and out of sight.

"Come on." He prodded Mick down the path with the tip of his gun.

I hurried past the building with the other two in my group, keeping far enough away that I could barely see anything. A growl brought my attention to the dead that were wandering through the woods.

A gun would have alerted Vinnie's group that we were there, so I took hold of my gun, swinging the butt into the almost dead person's head. Once it was on the ground, I plunged my knife into the squishy flesh, upwards toward the brain.

"Crap!" Now I had a knife that was icky and nothing to wipe it on. Great, another pair of jeans ruined.

We drifted in from the far side and were hiding just out of sight when Dad and Mick approached the door.

It opened, and the guy on duty wasn't expecting to see Dad with Mick, but a quick shot rang out, silencing him.

Dad's group pulled up out front and busted in the front door as this was going on so that no one tried to escape.

Vinnie walked out with Dad holding a gun to his head. "If he does anything, shoot. Everyone else needs to put down your guns and come outside.

The other two groups helped round everyone up, but the three of us were the backup in case someone else wasn't in the building, but had hidden in the woods.

All five of Vinnie's other guys, and Mick, were

lined up on their knees with their hands behind their heads.

"Look, we've just been trying to survive out here now that things are so messed up. If we didn't do what Vinnie said, he'd kill us and our families," one of the guys whimpered, earning a vicious look from Vinnie.

"What are the names of your family?" Dad questioned quickly.

"Dianne, Zach, and Ellie," he responded with no hesitation.

"Take him over to the side," Dad ordered.

The others all started saying names of their family members at once.

"Quiet. Mick, who's telling the truth?"

Eyes wide, Mick started to stutter.

Vinnie elbowed Ted and grabbed his gun, shooting Mick and the other four who were kneeling before my shot took him by surprise.

"What the hell?" Vinnie yelled, dropping the gun to grab his arm.

"Oh, did we forget to mention that we had shooters in the woods? Our bad. Thanks for taking out the trash and making the decision easier." Dad grinned, aiming the gun at Vinnie's head.

"Wait, you can't shoot me. I can give you all the

women that you want and all of our supplies," Vinnie pleaded.

"You're right, we'll take all the women and your supplies, but that's because we're going to free them from your reign of terror." Dad grabbed him by the back of the head and pulled until he had his attention. "I can shoot anyone I please who mistreats humans and executes other people because he's a snake."

He pulled the trigger, and Vinnie's head exploded, causing me to flinch.

Vinnie had to die, but I felt sad for the other guys that might have had families.

The one that was still alive couldn't talk fast enough. "I'm Kyle, and I'll take you to the camp so we can get the women and children free. A few of Vinnie's men will give you some trouble and will have to be taken out, but I can tell you on the way."

"Are there any more hiding in the woods, or anywhere else that we need to worry about?" Doug demanded.

"No, there's another group farther south than us in Georgia that Vinnie had contacted, and he was talking about trading some of the girls in exchange for supplies. I don't think they're an immediate threat, but if someone doesn't contact them in the next two weeks, they might come up here looking for our group," Kyle warned.

"So Vinnie was scared of this group?" Dad asked.

"Yeah. Well, he played the tough guy, but he was willing to give them whatever they wanted so the rest of us didn't die." A frown took over his face.

"One thing at a time. Let's rescue everyone and see how it goes from there. Kyle, you can ride with me," Dad offered.

Even though they were the bad guys, we all pitched in and dug a grave to put them in so that they weren't just lying around for the dead to eat on.

This wasn't exactly what the girls and I had in mind when we left this morning, and there were still farms that needed filled with workers.

"Dad, wait a second," I called out, hurrying to catch up.

"Yeah. What's up, honey?"

"If the guys in each group can handle it, there are several farms that need to have people taking care of the animals that are still alive. Sarah Beth was going to contact her uncle but we never made it there. I know that we don't want outsiders on the mountain until they've had a chance to prove themselves. Wouldn't this be a good way to let them do that and solve another problem at the same time?" I suggested.

"Wow, you've grown up so much. That would be great. I don't know how many people we have coming, but could you swing by and get the other girls? They'll be helpful in sorting this out since we've only got you and one other woman out here. I'm sure they'll feel more comfortable seeing other women that aren't as threatening as guys with guns." He threw an arm around my shoulders.

"No problem. I'm sure River is pacing already, hating that she's missing the action. See you in a bit." I headed for one of the trucks, excited that he hadn't only trusted me, but that he had let me go alone.

Which seemed like a good idea until I pulled up at the front gate and the one idiot that could make a problem was on duty.

"Clayton, can you open up so that I can get a few people to go help my dad?" I leaned out the window, waving, so that he'd lower the gun he had aimed at me.

He raised it slightly over the truck and fired.

I instinctively ducked, muttering, "What the hell?"

"It's me...Andi. Hello, my dad is Dawson. You know who I am!" I yelled, not caring who heard me at this point.

"I know, but I don't have orders to open the gate for anyone except my superior. I'm supposed to run off people who don't actually live here."

I crawled out the passenger door and rolled down the slight incline, out of sight.

Catching him off-guard, I ran at him, aiming for his knees because there was no way I could take down someone twice my size in a fair fight. His large frame made him think that he could take on anyone he wanted.

He let out a large 'oof', dropping the gun.

As I lay there on my back, I heard the footsteps of several people running up to the gate.

"What happened?" River cried, seeing me lying there as Clayton scrambled to his knees for his gun. "Andi, are you hurt?"

Emma wasn't far behind her, and others were scurrying up to see what was happening.

"I'm fine, as long as Clayton doesn't shoot at me again." I sat up, holding my side, trying to catch my breath from running and tackling him.

"Clayton, you shot at Andi? You've known her for years." His wife, Kelly, shook her head incredulously.

He just shrugged. "She tackled me and could have broken my back."

"Did you identify yourself? He might not have recognized you."

"Seriously, Kelly? He heard me and shot over the truck, even though I told him twice to open up, and even used Dad's name. He told me he didn't have orders from the boss to open up to anyone who didn't actually live here."

The gate had opened, and everyone was standing around in a circle, waiting.

"We've been checking everyone before we let them in so that the other group didn't sneak in to take one or all of us hostage," Kelly clarified, trying to justify her husband's actions.

"No, Clayton just wanted to throw his weight around. He knew exactly what he was doing. I'm so tired of your attitude, and I haven't even been 'living here.'" I walked over and poked him in the chest.

"I think it's about time that you were put on manure duty out in the fields," Emma insisted, knowing it would piss him off more if she spoke up.

"Now that's not fair that you get to decide what happens when you're one of the newest members here, Emma. I'm sure he feels bad about it, and that's kind of a harsh punishment," Kelly snapped.

"Ha! Do you see him apologizing to me? No, because he wanted to cause trouble, Kelly. He wants to be in charge and can't take it if a woman actually stands up to him. Why do you think Brad let Emma get involved when he's standing right there?" I crossed my arms, waiting for him to speak up.

Kelly glanced between Emma and Brad standing there, grinning behind her.

"Clayton, is there any way that you..." She trailed off when he gave her a nasty look.

"I'm not going to apologize or shovel shit. I'm tired of being taken advantage of, and nobody appreciates all the nights I've spent taking my turn for guard duty. All of you take the word of some military dudes who let women take charge instead of putting them where they belong. Kelly, get the kids. We're leaving." He grabbed her arm and started pulling her past the gate to the house.

"Clayton, we'll die out there. The kids won't survive against those things," Kelly tearfully protested.

"I can take care of my own family. I don't need all these others to do my job. I should've stayed in the city where there aren't so many leaders." Clayton tightened his grip when she stopped walking, and continued to drag her to where their kids were playing.

"No. We won't go out there." Kelly yanked her arm free and crossed them in a rare moment of defiance.

"You're my wife and I say go, so that's what we're gonna do." His six-foot frame towered over her, causing her to cringe.

Everyone was staying back and letting them work it out, unless he tried to actually hurt her. It was up to her to make this decision.

"I'm a Jackson first, and if you're dead, then it doesn't matter what you think because I won't be your wife anymore. If you go out there, you'll be dead in a week. You can't make it alone. The kids won't stand a chance, and I'm not going to make the choice of killing my kids or letting you commit suicide by zombie." Kelly's voice shook, but she straightened her back, gaining confidence.

"You'll do what I say," he threatened.

"No, that's where you're wrong. She's told you what's going to happen, and I suggest that you grab a pack, some bullets, and scram before Dawson gets back. If he finds out that you shot at Andi, even just a warning shot, he'll do what all of us really want to do," Brad warned, taking a stand next to Kelly.

"Really. And what is it that all of you really want to do to me? Huh?" Clayton moved toward Brad's face.

"Well, I for one would love to see that smile taken off your face. Everyone here has put up with your crap for years because we love Kelly, but we're done. Just because she made a bad choice, doesn't mean that she has to keep making it." I moved to her other side, and the others crowded behind us in a large show of strength.

Seeing the people that were ready to fight him if he pushed the issue, he threatened, "I'll get back at you for this. No one likes to be humiliated, and you'll be the second one on my list after I take care of my wife." He picked up the pack that had been brought out during the exchange.

"Good riddance," Emma muttered as he made his way out of the gate.

"You know we're going to have to be very careful. He knows how to sneak back in and hurt Kelly," I added, sliding an arm around her. "It's not her fault that her husband is horrible."

"I'll put everyone on alert, and we'll add a few extras that Dawson and I have been working on for things just like this," Brad reassured me.

"Sarah Beth, River, don't be mad at me. I suggested to Dad that we take the rescued ladies to some of the farms in the area. Depending on what Dad finds over there will determine what we need, and if there's still room for those up in Bethel," I reasoned.

"That makes sense, and if these ladies have been with Vinnie's gang for a while, they're going to need someplace to recuperate. Taking care of animals is a good way to do that," Sarah Beth agreed.

"We need to get going if we're going to get these ladies settled in before dark. We've been at this all day." I rubbed a hand wearily through my hair.

"I'm going back up to tell Angie where we're going to be, so that if Billy wakes up, she can tell him that we'll be back in the morning." Sarah Beth went up the paved road toward the medical cabin.

"Carson will need to be informed as well. He really wants us to take him back to his family. It'll have to be tomorrow, because I'm going to need some sleep after all that's happened today and last night." River started looking for the kids.

"Since you both have things to do, I'm going to say hi to Nana. If I don't, she might not let me back here to spend the night," I remarked, voicing the one thing that Clayton had correct, that I really didn't live there anymore.

The scariest thing about everything was that Vinnie's camp was only about ten miles away from the safety of our families. By the time we'd arrived, Dad and Kyle were explaining what had happened to Vinnie. A few of the other men were unhappy about it, but when Kyle explained that Vinnie had shot the others before his death, no one seemed really upset.

"Ladies, are we glad to see you. They have the women and children held in a couple of cages over there. Any time the men try to come over there, none of the women will leave because they're certain it's a trap. Can you talk to them so they'll believe you?" Doug pleaded with us.

"Of course. That's just horrible." Sarah Beth began walking in their direction. "Hey, now." She opened the locked door and pointed to me and River. "We're here to help you. Would you like to get away from here and go someplace safe? What's your name?"

"I'm Dianne. Kyle said we're free, but the last time one of our men said that, it was just a game for us to leave so they could chase us. They wanted to hunt us and see if we could outlast them and the zombies. You're for real, though? No extra punishments or night long visits?" Dianne gripped the fence with her fingers.

"It's not a game or a joke. Most of those men are dead. The question is, do all the guys need to die for all of you to feel safe again?" River wanted to reassure them, but knew that forced or not, the guys weren't completely innocent.

"Most of our husbands didn't do any of the raping, just the sadistic ones. Stay here." Dianne motioned to the others. "I'll point out the ones that weren't as bad as the others and make sure it's really okay."

She came out of the cage and walked between us. "I really want to take off running and find where they put my children."

Doug had lined all the men up, and was getting some information from each of them.

"Do you see any of the rest that aren't good?" Sarah Beth stood close, but gave her enough room to breathe.

"Out of the ten that are there, two of them are evil. The one in the middle and second from the end. The others went out today, and I don't see any of them here."

"Other than Kyle, the others that went out are all dead," River informed her. "I know that doesn't take away from what they did to you, but at least you can have a little peace that they won't do it to you again."

"Do you know where the other group of children are?" Dianne asked, puzzled when she didn't see any other cages.

"We haven't found anyone else here, and Kyle only mentioned the three cages over there," I acknowledged sadly.

"Ask King over there. He was the last one to see them. I don't have much hope he kept them alive, but I'd rather know the truth than to always be wondering." Dianne sniffled and turned back to the cages.

"I'll let my dad know and pull the trucks up here so you ladies can reunite with your children. We're taking you somewhere for the night, and not telling the men where you're at until tomorrow." I wanted to put her and the others at ease.

Dad saw me coming and walked away from Doug and the others. "Did we find out anything?"

"King and his buddy there are the only ones who know where Kyle and Dianne's kids are. They could still be alive. We'll have them loaded up shortly and be out of here, but we don't want to leave anyone behind," I informed him, unhappy with the facts I had.

"Okay. Take them out of here, and if we find the kids, I'll bring Kyle with them to where Dianne's staying." He frowned at the thought of kids being harmed.

"I've got it. Thanks, Dad." I couldn't resist the urge to hug him.

"What was that for?" He tilted his head, confused at my sudden display of affection.

"For not being an asshole and keeping me safe. I love you." While I didn't plan on dying anytime soon, I didn't want to leave it unsaid because I had taken a lot for granted before.

"You too, kiddo. I'm proud of you. Now, scoot so we can deal with these scumbags." He playfully mussed up my hair before going back to join Doug in his interrogation of Vinnie's gang.

We didn't have a vehicle that would transport passengers comfortably, but the women were so thankful to be free and have their children with them, that they weren't complaining at the conditions.

Dianne watched the other moms, a sad smile on her face.

"Are you okay?" I regretted the question as soon as it left my mouth. "Of course you're not okay."

"Don't worry about it. I'm just glad that there's

hope we'll live to see tomorrow. If my kids are alive, then I'll be even better. The others have their kids and that's bittersweet, but I'll make it." She pulled her hair out of her face as we picked up speed, falling silent.

With no problems, we made it back to the group of farms that we'd stumbled upon only a few hours earlier. Where had the day gone?

Sarah Beth and River had chosen the biggest place that could hold the most people.

"I know it's not a hotel, and it doesn't have running water, but at least it's clean and zombie free," River announced to the group as she parked.

"There's a tank with rainwater. If you want that we can bring it in, but I don't know if we can get it warmed up. I'm going out to see if I can get the pump on, if it's the same kind we have up the mountain." Sarah Beth, gun in hand, headed to the pasture where the well was located.

"Honestly, using the hose might be the best thing since most of us haven't had a bath in months. They weren't worried about hygiene, since food was the priority," Dianne offered, looking at the bedraggled group standing outside.

"What about clothes? They can't wear these rags after they get clean," River reminded me.

"Covered. When we left, I told Stacy to work with Nana and get some extras together. They're going to bring some things over, along with some warm food so that we don't have to worry about doing anything tonight." I was pleased that my family had been prepared enough that they could help others, even if the world was ending.

"Water's on!" Sarah Beth hollered from the well.

"Great. Boys and young men, if you can wash your hands with soap, then follow me please. We're going to go pick some fruit from the trees out there while these ladies get clean, and then we'll swap out. Buckets are in the barn for collecting fruit." River rounded them up and got them busy.

I went in the house and returned with a few unopened bottles of shampoo that had been in the cabinets, and all the towels. It wasn't the perfect setup, but it would work for now.

The ladies finally started chattering in small snatches, as the months of horror were washed away and they started to feel safe.

Hours later, after everyone was fed, clean, and huddled on the floors with blankets for the first time in a while, I sat on the porch with a shotgun perched in my lap.

The guys had never shown up, but that meant it wasn't safe for them to come to the house.

After being in the city for the past month, the country air seemed so different and quiet. We hadn't been able to restore power to everything yet, but the hum of motors could be heard more often than previously.

The zombies might have invaded our world, but the crickets still chirped in the stillness. A wolf's howl filled the air as Dianne joined me on the porch.

"I don't think I'll be able to go back to the way it was before. I became so numb, trying not to feel when they took us out of the cages. It's going to take forever to become somewhat normal again. Although, feeling clean is much better, and one step closer to that goal." She rubbed her arms nervously.

"Time to let your body heal and soak up the peace away from all those evil guys. Our family will help with that, and we're working with a church to stamp out this zombie population. Things are closer to returning to normal than you think." I sat up, because there was movement at the tree line, and there weren't any accompanying growls, so it was something alive.

I brought the gun up so that I could use the scope my dad had given me for night vision.

Someone was struggling with two ZITs, but was taking them out. I was trying to adjust for a closer look at the person's face when I felt a sting hit my shoulder.

"Andi, what is it?" Dianne cried out next to me as I crumpled to the ground. "Crap! Someone shot you."

Without hesitation, she picked up the shotgun from my unresisting hands and aimed at the intruder.

Two shots rang out, bringing, River, Stacy, and Sarah Beth from inside where they were sleeping.

"Someone shot Andi, but he's down right now. Be careful, there were zombies out there that he killed before shooting her," Dianne warned, as River took off running to the tree line.

Sarah Beth dropped to her knees beside me. "Andi, can you hear me?"

All I could do in response was groan. If I opened my mouth, a scream would have come out instead of words.

Dianne produced a flashlight from somewhere, and Sarah Beth's gasp told me that the wound was bad.

"Dianne, go to the kitchen and put a pot of water

onto the fire. We're going to need clean water to clean things up so you don't get infected. Then bring me any rags or towels that look clean," she ordered.

"I'll get the towels," River volunteered, out of breath from running back to us. "Andi, it was Clayton. He's dead."

Sarah Beth might not have had medical training, but she knew what do with a gunshot wound. There weren't many doctors up in Bethel, and self-care was the only thing standing between those in life-threatening situations.

"We're going to get you patched up and run you over to Angie. She'll have supplies to keep you alive. It looks like it went straight through." She took the towels from River and applied pressure.

"Agh!" I cried through gritted teeth, trying not to make too much noise.

"It doesn't look like it hit an artery, but you're still bleeding excessively." She removed the first set of towels and put another in place, wrapping a curtain around the padding to keep it in place.

"Who's going to take her over there? We really need someone to watch her and be on the lookout in case Clayton wasn't the only out there. I don't want to leave everyone alone here and unprotected." River stood back, out of Sarah Beth's way.

"I'll go with Sarah Beth. I can drive in case Andi needs me. I know a couple of the ladies who would be glad to help," Dianne chimed in from the doorway.

"You won't need the water now since we don't have to clean anything to dig it out, but we don't want to wait too long," Stacy advised, hovering over me with the others.

"Just take me to Angie. If anyone can help me, it'll be Sarah Beth and Angie. Please, it hurts like a…" I closed my eyes, hearing their voices, but not really caring anymore.

Chapter 11

River

I was certain that we were going to lose Andi. Cole was going to be so mad that he hadn't had a chance to kill the asshole himself. There was no way to let him know that Andi was hurt yet.

Dawson drove up the driveway with the other nine men from Vinnie's group, and I hated to be the one to tell him what was going on.

"I see that you made it. Gentlemen, we ask that you go out back to the partitioned area and use the hose. There's a table with clothes we saved for you." I pointed around to the back, and the men went without a word.

"Something's wrong. What happened?" Dawson demanded, picking up on my nervousness.

"Follow me." Bat in hand, I went out to where I'd made sure that Clayton wasn't going to get up again.

"We had an incident last night. Someone was out here and killed a couple of ZITs. He then shot at us before Dianne returned fire and killed him. I made sure that he and the others weren't going to get up."

"Why are you showing me?" Dawson registered who was lying on the ground as he asked the needless question. "I don't understand what was he doing out here. We only had you girls on lookout duty."

"Yep, there was a problem on Jackson Mountain yesterday when Andi came to get us. He shot at her and started threatening us. Kelly stood up to him and he was kicked off the mountain. We think he followed Stacy when she brought us dinner." I laid a hand on his arm. "That's not all, though."

"Andi...where's Andi?" He began to panic when he realized that his daughter, not me, should have been the one giving him the report.

"He shot her. She was alive when Sarah Beth took her over to Angie. The bullet went through, and we don't think it hit anything major."

Dawson started pacing back and forth, landing a well-placed kick every time he got near Clayton's body.

"Always knew he's be trouble when Kelly first brought him around us."

"Dawson, what happened?" Doug asked as he approached. "Oh, crap. Is everyone all right?" He looked back and forth between us.

"They took Andi to the house."

"That's what they told me. So what are we waiting for?" Doug started back toward the house, but stopped when Dawson didn't follow him.

"We can't go over there yet. These guys need some help getting setup, and my pacing will just get in the way," Dawson growled.

"She's your kid, though. I think everyone will understand," I consoled.

"Nope. We need to work, and that's where my efforts are best used. The guys should be clean by now, and it'll be easier to sort them out." Dawson stopped pacing and took off at a near run to the house.

"Yeah, he should, but in a way, he's right. We can use his extra energy to accomplish a lot today in making these people feel secure," I agreed.

"Time will tell, and they would have called us on the radios if she hadn't made it. Speaking of that, did you find Dianne and Kyle's children?"

"Yes, and no. We know that they're alive, but they were the down payment on the supplies that Vinnie got last week from the group in Georgia." Doug winced.

"Oh, that's sucky. Dianne's going to be so frustrated."

"Let's get this done so we can get Dawson back over there quickly.

"Agreed."

Hours later, all three farms had three families and a few singles staying there. No electricity made things difficult, and I had an idea about that, but at least they had some fresh fruit and vegetables from the gardens. Most farms this far from the cities had some form of heat that didn't rely on electricity for warmth or cooking food.

"We're going to let each one of you take care of your own group, and we'll check in on you to help make sure things go smoothly. There's another group farther down south, and they have some kids who need to be rescued. We don't know much about them or how big they are, but they'll be looking for a meet up in the next two weeks," Dawson explained to the group before we loaded them up to take to the other two farms.

"There are several fields and orchards that need to be harvested, and we're working on finding more people to help, and even get another crop in before winter starts. The Church Against Zombies group is hoping that we can get an interstate co-op going before winter hits," I assured everyone.

"Any place that has the possibility of food and shelter without hurting our families is wonderful," Peggy replied. "We don't mind working to survive, especially if we're working for ourselves."

"A lookout will be setup so that if a group comes up from the south, we'll know about it. Even though you're safe right now, remember that there are still ZITs out there, so don't go out without taking precautions until we get lights setup. Nobody outside after dark," Doug added.

"We'll leave you to it. Kyle is going with us to talk to Dianne, and they'll be by to check on everything before dark hits." Dawson was getting antsy about seeing Andi.

"You go take care of your kid. We appreciate everything you've done for us." Gene hugged his wife.

"If one of you will get sizes of clothes, I'll bring back a truckload with me when the guys come to install the electric." I figured it couldn't hurt if they had more than one outfit to wear at a time.

"Oh, clean bodies and a change of clothes is just amazing." Peggy left her husband's side and gave me a hug.

"Um, sure. No problem. The clothes are just going to waste sitting in the stores, so we might as well make good use of them." I patted her back awkwardly. "Ready?" I asked, extracting myself from her embrace.

"Yeah, hop in the truck. We're only going to take one back so they have some form of transportation," Doug interjected.

Now that we were driving toward Andi, Dawson wasn't wasting any time, and the suggested speed limit for a law-abiding citizen was definitely being broken.

The twenty-minute drive took closer to ten, and since Doug had radioed ahead, the gate was open for us.

Dawson was out the door and running up the hill to the medical cabin.

The rest of us that were left got out at a much slower pace.

"It's a good thing he doesn't do the driving very often because I think I might be sick," I groaned, staggering out of the truck and leaning against a tree.

"Some of the guys in the military should be in Nascar races, or join a street gang because there wasn't room for that kind of driving before the zompoc, much less afterward," Doug commented as he held his stomach and weaved toward the house with Stacy holding onto her brother.

I walked up the hill to see how Andi was, and found myself next to Carson.

"How's it going, kid?" I was genuinely glad to see him.

"Pretty good. Billy's sort of better. He can actually talk coherently again. That other girl, Andi? She's been out since they brought her in last night," Carson informed me.

"I'm glad to hear that. Maybe we can take you home tomorrow. What do you think?"

"Whoo!" he yelled, and then put a hand over his mouth. "Sorry."

"Perfectly understandable, kid. Your mom will be excited to see you."

We got to the cabin, and Angie joined us outside, taking a seat on the steps.

"River, your group needs to slow down and quit bringing me injured people. I had enough to do already with running my own medic school. We didn't need real life people to work on," Angie teased.

"Can we send someone to train, and then we won't have to come back and forth from such a great distance?"

"Tell those geeks over there to get the internet up and working so we can learn from the tube know-it-all channel. A couple of people learning and doing practical application should help, but in some ways, it's going to be a mix of old-school and new school until we get life back to normal."

"That would a nice change. This isn't a bad alternative, and I kind of like the view most days." Her gaze was focused on Doug walking between two buildings.

"Oh, I see. What does Stacy think of that development?"

"Happy for him. He's never had a chance to settle down, and it's not like I'm going anywhere. Heard that you might've found yourself one of the trio of cousins. Last one to fall, and they generally go down the hardest when they take the plunge." Angie eyed me carefully. "You don't seem to have that 'just fell in love' glow. Don't you miss him?"

"That's a good question. I do miss having him around, but we've just started something, and I'm not even sure what that is exactly. I'm not really one of those gushy types, and I don't know what the next step is." I shrugged.

"Just take his cue. He'll either be happy to see you, or he'll be so pissed off that it won't matter, and you'll get to have hot make-up sex. Really, either way, you should get hot make-up sex. It'll just be a few degrees hotter if he's mad than if he's just happy to see you," Angie advised.

"Sounds like you've been around the block a few times."

"A few." She grinned. "Dillion's dad was a bad boy. We would fight, and the make-up was great, but then one day he just left. I had a baby and had to support both of us, so other than the occasional date, I've stayed single."

"Sounds like it's time for a change, and you've already got your eye one someone. I'll take it one moment at a time and see how Cole's feeling when I get back. I feel like we've done something bad and snuck out. He might not forgive us when he finds out that Andi's been shot."

"He will. She's going to pull through. It might be a week or two before she goes back to the city, but she'll make a full recovery," Angie promised. "Wanna go in and see her?"

"Sure. I'll bet she's ready to get rid of Dawson for a few minutes."

With our goodbyes said, we loaded up some fresh food supplies and Carson's truck with the alcohol to take to his mom.

Stacy was the only one going back with me at the moment, because Sarah Beth needed to make contact with Bethel and get them down the mountain to help.

It looked like we'd be coming back and forth a little more often to get fresh food and bring back stuff that the new community needed.

I was driving Carson in his truck, and hoped that he would remember where he lived. It had only taken a few extra days, but the improvement with Billy was still on the fence, and Angie wanted to keep him a little longer. Hopefully, the co-op Carson talked about would be willing to do some trade as well. If Billy was doing better, then I'd be able to drive him home on the next trip through.

"We looked on the map, and I think we found the town you came from. Do you think if we get close enough, you'll be able to find it if we're in the general area?" The wind blowing through the window felt really good in the early morning sun.

"Yeah, but we should meet one of the lookouts before we get there. They're posted on all the major roads. We bypassed them by going on a few backroads."

"Ah, that explains a few things about how this all happened," I responded, keeping an eye on Stacy behind me.

This was the most exposed we'd been in a while, and I was on alert because this was uncharted territory.

About thirty minutes later, the road was blocked and I slowed down. "Do the lookouts know you?" All I could see were a few men with guns trained on us.

"Ma'am, how can we help you?" A guy approached the car while the others moved into a position to cover us.

"I came across Carson here and he was lost. I'm looking for his mom, Trish, and her sister, Jessica. Oh, and a guy named Linc. Do you know them? Can you help us?" I figured I'd approach it like I would have before the zombies and just ask for directions.

"Did she say Carson? Where are the other missing kids?" One of the other guys came to stand by the window.

"If your Carson, then your mom's going to have your hide. We've been looking for weeks, and most of us were certain that you were dead."

"That's kind of the problem. He went with these

other kids and things got a little crazy. He didn't know how to get home because he hasn't lived on the farm that long. Could one of you point us in the right direction?" At least they seemed to believe us and lowered their guns.

"Move the barricade," he hollered to the others before turning back to me. "I'll get in my truck and you can follow me. I can't take the chance that you'd get lost."

"Sure. He's anxious to let his mom know what happened." Relieved, I followed the truck and was struck by the difference after we crossed the barricade. As we drove by fields, there were people out working, and children playing like before people were infected by zombies.

"That next road we should take a right, and it's a few miles down past the next cross section. Oh, thank goodness." Carson wiped at his face, trying to hide his emotions.

"Wonderful. Just remember that when your mom yells at you, it's because she loves you and thought you weren't coming back. Take whatever punishments she hands out, and remember that it's her way of trying to keep you safe. Okay?"

He nodded, twisting his hand nervously. "She'll still love me, right?"

My heart broke at hearing his doubt. "I never had a mom, but from what I've heard, they're pretty forgiving and love you, even when you screw up. Give her a chance, and you'll quickly know where you stand."

The truck in front of us slowed down and signaled a turn. Old habits from before still gave glimpses of the past life.

"This is it." Carson got excited.

A gate opened, and the guy in the truck had an animated conversation with the guard, causing them to radio ahead.

"Here comes Linc." Carson hopped out and ran around the truck before I could stop him.

"Carson!" Linc yelled and gave him a huge hug. "Your mother is going to be so excited. Run on up to the house."

As he turned Linc lose, a group came out and met him about halfway. Seeing that Carson was taken care of, Linc turned his attention to me.

I left the gun in the truck and got out slowly.

"Linc? I'm River." I held out my hand as he approached. "We found him and Billy in a cabin, almost starved to death."

"Billy? You have Billy as well?" He examined the

trucks for signs of another kid.

"Not exactly. We found Billy, but he'd broken his leg and it was an open wound. It had been infected and gotten gangrene, so we had to amputate it. Our nurse got him moved and antibiotics into him. He was incoherent when we found them. This morning, he was talking and looking much better, but Angie thought we shouldn't move him yet. She wanted to give him about a week." I spoke in a rush so that he wouldn't reach the wrong conclusion.

"He's alive. That's wonderful, and you have a nurse? Where are you from?" he asked suspiciously.

"I think that's a discussion we should have after you've talked to Carson and get his take on our treatment of them." I motioned to the truck. "He found the alcohol and we brought it all to you, minus the bottle we used on Billy."

Ignoring my overture to talk, he walked over and looked around the trucks. After a thorough examination, he came back, appearing satisfied.

"Drive on up to the house." He accepted my story, motioning over to the guy who had brought us. "Thanks for your help, Brent."

"Glad we found them, Linc." Brent waved as he backed out, heading back to the barricade.

I had barely put the truck in park before Carson came running over to hug me. "She still loves me. We cried, and she's not going to let me out of her sight ever again."

Grinning ruefully at the woman hovering behind Carson, I said, "I thought that might be the case. You must be the mom who still loves him. I'm River, and this is Stacy."

"Thank you for bringing my son home." She came toward me, and I was suddenly being hugged again.

"You're welcome. Sorry, I'm not used to hugs." I wiggled to get out of the extra affection.

"I'm sorry, where are my manners?" She laughed. "Please, come inside. We have lemonade. This is my sister, Jessica, and her significant other, Linc, who you've already met. Carson, you may stay in the yard, but I want to be able to see you from the window," she warned him.

"Yes, Mom." He nodded happily. "I'll stay with the kids. I missed them."

They waited until he was out of earshot. "Who are you two, and how do you look so clean and healthy?"

Countless questions later, Stacy and I had retold the story to all three adults. We had permission from Brad and Dawson to tell them about the other two groups. I had also argued over telling them what had happened with Vinnie's group.

"They didn't want to worry you with something we'd taken care of, but I felt this needed to be said. Vinnie's group isn't the only one out there that may try to attack us. He did some trading with a southern group out of Georgia, who are expecting to meet next week. We're taking precautions, but they could suddenly show up, and I believe that your barricade guards should be warned." I had gotten close to Carson, and didn't want anything to happen to his family.

"The Church Against Zombies that River and I are associated with have been trying to put things back together again. We're working with those on Jackson Mountain to get the farms and harvests done. We're looking for a way to trade with each community, and I'm impressed that you have a ZIT free zone," Stacy complemented them.

I interrupted her moment of kissing up. "What she's trying to say is, that we have a few farms with new residents that could use some help with solar panels so they have water and electric. Is there any way that you could help install some for us?"

"We've been planning to make contact with the Church Against Zombies group that we heard on the radio, but when the kids went missing, we switched priorities. We've had some people installing panels in the other towns, and the rest of us have been clearing out a wider area toward your mountains in hopes that we would find the kids." Linc shook his head in frustration. "If you don't mind, I'd like to go with you and see the setup there. I won't be going in blind, and we won't have to bring an entire group as backup since you ladies obviously check out."

"Our guys will take what we have to say and run with it. Carson is a special kid, and he couldn't have turned out like he is if you were horrible people," I acknowledged.

"Well, you didn't have to bring Carson back or help Billy. That speaks volumes, and there's the fact that they sent two women into negotiations with another group that could have been really hostile. I would be honored to see if we can make something work. I'm ready to get the world back to normal."

"On that note, would it be possible to use your bathroom before we leave? And I'd like to say goodbye to

Carson if that's all right." I looked at his mother for confirmation.

"Absolutely."

"Oh, and he was very worried that you weren't going to love him anymore. He's your kid, and I know you have to come up with some sort of punishment, but he did keep himself and another kid alive for weeks. He also buried his friends, and in my book, that's a pretty horrible thing to go through at his age. I don't have kids, but just thought I'd put a good word in for him."

"Don't worry, he'll be doing chores and sleeping on a mattress in my room for a while. My boy isn't even that anymore. He's grown into a man in the last few months." Trish started to hug me again, but remembered my comment earlier.

"I'd like to make it through to the safe zone before dark if you don't mind. It's been a long few days, and there's a guy that needs to be told the girl he likes got shot."

"Of course. I'll just get my pack." Linc kissed Jessica and walked to the back of the house, and was back within ten minutes.

"We'll ride together, but you can take the lead until we get to the edge of Knoxville," I offered, so he didn't feel uncomfortable riding with someone he didn't know for hours on end.

He nodded. "Sounds good. Let's get on the road."

Chapter 12

River

The closer we got to the church, the more nervous I became about seeing Cole again. I wasn't having the same thoughts as Carson had been, but I was worried at the same time.

Our blockades were more to keep the infected from coming through than the people, but that would be changing due to our run-ins with Vinnie's group.

When I pulled up to the business that we'd established aboveground for bringing new people in, there he was, leaning against the doorjamb.

"Now or never, River. You can do this. Just fake it till you make it, right?" I mumbled as I got out.

"Well, well, look what the cat dragged in." Cole smiled.

"Aw, crap. He's smiling, and that isn't good." I didn't have any witty comebacks.

"Linc Harris, the world is a small place. I see you found our girls and brought them back to us." Cole engulfed his friend in a backslapping hug.

"You have got to be shitting me."

Stacy ignored me, as she was welcomed back with a breathtaking kiss from Darren.

"Oh, I'd love to take credit for these ladies, but they're the ones who found our missing kid. He's been gone for three weeks, and they just drove right up with him. Then they told us about what you guys were doing over here, and I had to come see if we could find a way to work together," Linc informed Cole.

"At least they survived the two full days they were gone," Cole growled toward me.

"Hey, I'm just glad they're back. I missed this lady. She's growing on me." Darren kept his arm around Stacy as he shook hands with Linc. "Don't mind Cole, he's been cranky because he can't keep this one on a leash. She's independent and does her own thing."

"It does seem to be a problem, but I've gotten used to independent women like my niece. We're missing two people, Andi and Sarah Beth." Cole scanned my face, and didn't like what he was seeing.

"Let's do this inside, it's a long story. Lee and Sean also need to hear what I have to say. They're safe, so don't worry." I ducked the question and walked inside as he pulled out a phone.

"Send Lee and Sean over to the processing station please. We need their help with a situation." Cole continued to glower while joking around with Linc.

Lee came racing in the door, gun held to his side, not wanting to shoot someone.

"What's the hurry?" Sean arrived at a much slower pace.

"We ran into a couple situations," I began, "but we lost a few people in the process. Sarah Beth is fine, but Andi got shot."

"She's fine," Stacy said calmly. "Clayton isn't, though. One of the ladies we rescued shot him. He's dead."

"Holy crap!" Cole landed heavily in the chair behind him. "What did you girls do, start a revolution and get caught in the crossfire?"

"Our intention was to make some paths out into the rural areas and see if we could find some food sources. We stumbled upon Carson and Billy, which led to us being attacked by another rogue group." I felt my confidence coming back. "Don't start with how you could have saved us if you'd been there. We did just fine on our own," I admonished Cole.

"Obviously you did," he shot back, unimpressed.

"Give them a break. You haven't heard the rest yet." Linc joined in, giving me the floor again.

"We took out the other group, and in the process, Clayton shot at Andi. Kelly finally stood up to him, and we escorted him off the mountain. Evidently, he followed one of the groups bringing supplies and tried to take us out at the farm. One of the ladies we rescued took the gun when Andi fell, and shot him."

"Dawson did really well and didn't flip out," Stacy added.

"Well, if you don't count his pacing and kicking the dead body every time he passed." I laughed at the expression on the men's faces. "Hey, if he'd taken a shot at my kid, I'd have done the same thing, as would all of you."

"I'd have mutilated his dead body," Cole fumed. "What, like you wouldn't have made sure that he was completely dead?"

"Anyway, she's fine and recovering. She and Billy should be able to start moving around in the next few days, and if there are no complications, they can each go home."

"Can I go see her?" Sean asked out of the blue.

"Um, we weren't going to make another trip until next week." Stacy frowned, looking at me to see what I thought.

"I have a better idea. Linc, is there any way that you could take Sean over there? You could take Billy's parents with you. Is there anything that you need for your community?" I offered.

"If we're going to make this trade thing work, we might as well start now, and from what you've said, they'll let Sean in, and it will be a huge relief for Billy's parents. We need more equipment and gas for the vehicles." Linc surveyed the room.

"I think that's a possibility. How much are you wanting right now?" Lee questioned.

"An entire truck for the filling station would be nice, but most of the farm equipment runs on diesel. We can install the solar panels that your farms need, and we have crops that have been producing," Linc explained.

"Once I see Andi, I can go and install the panels," Sean stated. "If you don't want to do a deal with this guy, or want to use the resources, I mean, it's what I can do."

"Linc's an old army buddy, and I'm not worried about his intentions. Getting the world back to what it was is going to take some effort, and with that comes an exchange of resources. Having another place with different food groups would be wonderful." Cole's expression wasn't as pained now that he'd heard the rest of the story.

"Sean, we knew that you'd want to head that way. Brad and Dawson need you and a couple of the geeks."

"Hey, I'm more than just my brains. I've got some brawn as well," Sean protested.

"Agreed. Andi must see something in you, and the rest of us will just have to wait to be wowed. Anyway, they need a system setup to warn if this group comes up from Georgia. We have to find a way that they won't come and take everything away that we've built," I teased him.

"Look, we all know that things aren't going the way we wanted them to, and certainly not how we thought the world would be. We've been locked in groups of people that have played by the rules, and so far, we've dealt with nice people. In just two short days, I've come across two very different types of horrible people. Ones that took advantage of those too weak to look out for themselves, and the other one wanted power and was willing to hurt others just to get it." I suddenly felt like crying. "Why don't you guys figure out the details, and I'm going to go check on something."

All the emotions and feelings of the past few days had just hit me, and I had to get away before I broke down.

I rounded the building and slid to the ground behind a dumpster, out of sight. What I didn't expect was for Cole to sit down next to me, holding my bat.

He didn't say anything, he just laid the bat down on the other side of me.

"I don't want you to see me like this," I groaned, my head hidden in my arms.

"River, you can hide from me, but you're not going to scare me off." He waved a hand to our surroundings. "These infected things are scary, but even they're not that bad compared to some stuff I've seen out there. You can put up walls to keep me and all these other people out, yet we're some of the nice ones who actually care."

He put an arm around me, pulling me closer to him. "I know that we aren't dating, or that we haven't had a moment to discuss what we are. I was a little pissed."

I gave him a disbelieving look.

"Yeah, okay. I was really pissed. Darren talked with me and Lee. They both were fine with what you girls did, running off. Then I realized that I was used to being part of a group, and even though I feel like we really know each other, you might feel rushed into something. It's not like you can just go home and chill. We all live and work in the same space. So I'm not mad. But next time, I would appreciate a heads-up." His finger lifted my chin up so that my face wasn't hidden by my hair. "Can we at least agree to be partners?"

With an offer like that, I couldn't say anything, but I reached up and brought his head down so that our lips touched in a gentle kiss.

"Thank you. I appreciate that you're giving me space." I snuggled into his arm, enjoying the moment. "This is just me having a weak moment. I won't be into cuddling on a regular basis," I informed him. "So don't get any ideas that I won't push all the boundaries in this relationship, because that's kind of my specialty."

"That's what I'm counting on, Pumpkin."

Instead of a comeback, I just gave him a loving slap on the back of the head. "Don't call me pumpkin." I grinned at him. "In public," I clarified. "Now, I want to see what you've been doing with yourself while I've been gone."

"Yes, ma'am. But when do we get to have the hot make-up sex?"

"Who said that make-up sex was on the table?" I countered.

"Well that's what you do when you have a fight, right?" He turned that devilish grin toward me.

"So I've been told, but I would need a much quieter and non-public space this time."

"Absolutely. Follow me to the make-up sex private space I've arranged."

"You sneaky devil."

"Only because you're my angel."

The End

Want to read more?

Read Now

A Word From the Author

If you enjoyed this story, please leave a review even if it is one short sentence. Do you want to know when the next book comes out or to get to know me better? Feel free to stalk me on all the social media sites. (No real-life stalking because that's just not cool.) Thanks for reading and I hope to hear from you.

-Alathia Paris Morgan

Newsletter signup:

Sign up Here for Zombie News: http://eepurl.com/dBkPiP

Author Facebook page:

http://www.facebook.com/apmorganbooks

Instagram:

http://www.instagram.com/alathiamg

Twitter:

http://www.twitter.com/alathiamg

Street Team:

https://www.facebook.com/groups/1442476186066361/

Website:

http://www.alathiamg.com

Goodreads:

https://www.goodreads.com/author/show/8611387.Alathia

Paris_Morgan

Bookbub:

https://www.bookbub.com/authors/alathia-paris-morgan

Sneak Peek

Geeks Against Zombies

Sean

I'd always thought Andi was a cute kid. One of the gang, and fun to hang out with. That was the only amount of effort I'd put into analyzing my sister's roommate. Then the zombies came out of nowhere, and my video games were a living thing in my world. Well, not really living, but undead, trying to kill us all.

My friends and I had it better than most, because we knew how to deal with this kind of situation. We had watched hundreds of movies about zombies, and while we were still the geeks that sat inside all day, that changed when the zombies showed up. Killing those things was the workout we needed to survive and get us out into the real world.

Survival became our main objective, and then the Church Against Zombies group showed up on our doorstep, bringing the one girl that I'd missed when the world went crazy—Andi.

Suddenly my skills for electronics were needed to put civilization back together, and Andi never left my side until the other ladies decided to go exploring without telling anyone. I'd never been so scared in my entire life.

When River and Stacy came back, bringing the news that Andi had been shot, the only thing I could think was, how fast can I get to her? I couldn't let her die without knowing I liked her as more than just a friend. I'm not sure if I'll get the chance now, because another group has plans to attack us and take what they want. The mountain groups need my help to get electricity going, and to setup a system to warn us of incoming intruders.

It's all so crazy, and I never thought that my game world would collide and take over my real life.

Printed in Poland
by Amazon Fulfillment
Poland Sp. z o.o., Wrocław